# Death of a Chancellor

# ALSO BY WARREN CARRIER

### NOVELS

*The Hunt*
*Bay of the Damned*

### POETRY

*The Cost of Love*
*Toward Montebello*
*Leave Your Sugar for the Cold Morning*
*The Diver*

### OTHER

*City Stopped in Time*
*Reading Modern Poetry*, Coeditor
*Guide to World Literature*, Editor
*Literature from the World*, Coeditor

# Death of a Chancellor

Warren Carrier

Dodd, Mead & Company
New York

Published by Dodd, Mead & Company, Inc.
79 Madison Avenue, New York, N.Y. 10016
Distributed in Canada by
McClelland and Stewart Limited, Toronto
Manufactured in the United States of America
Designed by Erich Hobbing
First Edition

*Library of Congress Cataloging-in-Publication Data*

Carrier, Warren Pendleton.
  Death of a chancellor.

  I. Title.
PS3505.A7736D35   1986      813'.52      86-2005
ISBN 0-396-08815-5

For Judy and Ethan
and Gregory

# Death of a Chancellor

# I

Silvertown, Wisconsin, is a small town in the northern part of the state in the midst of pine forests and lakes where the fishing and hunting are good and the only silver worth mentioning belongs to Nate Colby, chairman of the board of the First National Bank of Silvertown (and the Silvertown Telephone Company and the Silvertown Shopping Mall and the Silvertown Feed Mill). The Colbys and their occasional guests eat with it.

The Anaconda Company found copper ore (and, it is rumored, some other metals) in quantity under the ground not far from town, but the state, in its customary greed, hastened to place such a tax on processing the ore that the Anaconda Company—the price of copper depressed in any case—has not removed a spadeful of dirt to recover its find. The state, of course, continues to mine the income of its citizens at a rate second only to that of New York City.

Some of our tax money, however, returns to Silvertown in the form of the University of Wisconsin—Silvertown. The university is Silvertown's gold mine. This is not to say that all citizens are happy about having a small university in our midst; some, indeed, refer to our seat of learning as "that damned university." This, naturally, is not the view of progressive citizens, such as the members

1

of the Chamber of Commerce. The university pumps some sixteen million dollars annually into the local economy, and, as representatives of the university are wont to remind the Rotary Club, that money turns over several times and provides jobs for the citizens and profit for business. Without the university, Silvertown would doubtless consist of the feedmill, a service station, Clancy's Tavern, a superette, the Lutheran church, and the summer resort on Lake Arrowhead.

With the university, we have a population of ten thousand (not counting five thousand students) and we are the largest town in the area. There is even enough income and activity in town to support three law firms, one of which bears my name and those of my two partners: Fogarty, Svenson and Bosch. I'm Fogarty.

I'm a native of Silvertown; Svenson came from Lost Lake, nearby. We both went to the university here (it was then called Silvertown State College); I majored in English, Svenson in History. We got our law degrees from Madison. Bosch is a German Catholic from Milwaukee (pronounced "Mmwawkey") and got his B.A. and law degree from Marquette. I handle mostly real estate and probate and do such criminal trial work as comes our way; Svenson and Bosch do some real estate, divorces, and whatever else they can find. Our office is on Main Street at the corner of Second, over Clancy's Tavern.

All this is to explain why the death, the murder as it turned out, of the university chancellor was a pretty big event for us. Wisconsin being a small state, where everybody of any importance at all knows everybody else of any importance at all, it was not a small affair for the whole state. The *State Journal* in Madison and the Milwaukee papers, in fact, made it front-page news for three days, at first when the chancellor was discovered dead, and then when the autopsy disclosed he had been murdered.

2

I'm telling about myself (my curriculum vitae would scarcely be of interest otherwise) because shortly after we discovered that the chancellor had, indeed, been murdered, Hannah Train, wife of the late chancellor, came to me for help. Bill and Hannah and my wife, Susie, and I were fairly good friends, at first because I was on the Alumni Association Board and later because we liked each other—especially Hannah and Susie. Hannah came to me for help because the sheriff of Lost County (that's our county, no jokes, please) had begun to question her so persistently she had come to think he suspected she had done her husband in. Bill's death had hit Hannah pretty hard, and I was happy to help, by suggesting to Sheriff Anderson that he stop harassing her unless he was prepared to charge her with something, and, if the latter were the case, I would warn her not to say another word.

It was Susie who came up with the idea that, if I were to help Hannah and get the sheriff off her back, I should try to find out who, in fact, had committed the crime. Besides, I owed it to Bill, who had been a good friend.

"That's the job of the sheriff, the Silvertown Police, and the state, Susie," I said. "I'm not a cop; I'm a country lawyer."

We were having coffee on a Monday morning some ten days after the murder and four days after the funeral. Susie buys coffee beans in Madison whenever she gets down there and grinds some fresh every morning. Despite the fact that she, too, is a native of Silvertown, she's pretty quick. Besides, she got her degree at Madison. Why she came back to Silvertown with me so that I could practice law in our hometown is beyond me. Sometimes I'm lucky.

"Sean, I'm not suggesting you play Sherlock Holmes. You don't smoke a pipe or shoot up with cocaine, to begin with. But surely you could nose around enough to take the heat off Hannah. And, besides, who could it have been?

3

Who could posibly have wanted to kill Bill Train?" She had that look of determined concern on her pretty, freckled face I had learned I couldn't ignore.

"I don't know," I said. "Maybe some faculty member he didn't promote."

Susie pinched my biceps. "Don't be facetious."

"I'm not being," I said. "In any event, I doubt old Bert Anderson or Chief Dicky James would appreciate my nosing around like a county sheriff. And even if they didn't mind, I wouldn't know how to go about it or where to begin."

"If you insist on being facetious, you could begin with the faculty members who didn't get promoted this year," she said. She took a big bite of English muffin covered with her Aunt Sandy's strawberry preserves.

She looked good eating it. "Can I have another muffin?" I said.

"Are you going to help Hannah and poor Bill and find out who did it?"

"Who done it," I corrected. "And are you blackmailing me with an English muffin and Aunt Sandy's strawberry preserves?"

She got up to get me a muffin and kissed me on the cheek. "Yes, I am," she said. She put a muffin in the toaster.

"I'll think about it." I said.

I thought about it on the way to the office. I didn't have much confidence in Sheriff Anderson on a matter like this. He was better at catching speeders and poachers. I didn't know how deeply the state's Criminal Investigation Bureau would get involved. The murder of a chancellor might draw in some powerful investigative help. On the other hand, I was as curious as Susie about who had done it, and I knew everybody in town, more or less, and that included a lot of faculty members. (Somehow, when you thought

4

about the university and faculty members, you thought about them as though they were not part of the town.)

There were, inevitably, some people connected with the university who had not been happy with Bill Train. He had fired at least two deans and a coach and not reappointed a number of faculty members; he had been tough about standards for promotions and tenure, tough as well about student standards and behavior. Some faculty may have loved him; most, I knew, had respected him. He had not been the kind to have pals after the fashion of his dean of instruction. He had played no favorites on a personal basis. He had been warm and witty; and he had also, when it came to educational values, been as stern as a Lutheran minister.

He was very bright, an intellectual in a provincial university; he was a scholar and had published a fair amount in his field, which was philosophy. I never read any of his scholarly work (my tastes run to legal decisions on real estate and spy novels), but I understand it was respectable stuff. Of course, having a chancellor who was an intellectual and who published, even as an administrator, might not have pleased some faculty members who, having to teach all of twelve hours a week, complain they don't have time to be scholars.

As I thought about Bill and what Susie had suggested, I became more intrigued, and by the time I walked the ten brisk blocks through the cold spring air to my office, I decided to take a stab at it. Had I known then what I was getting into, I might well have stuck with working out the legal details for selling farm acreages and tracts of timber.

# II

All I had to begin with was what we all knew, what had appeared in the papers. The chancellor had gone to his office on Saturday morning as usual. This was the time of week he worked on his scholarly projects, when everything else was out of the way and there were seldom faculty or students about to intrude. When he didn't come home for lunch, as he almost always did, Hannah was a little concerned but not worried. He might have gone to the library. Whenever he went somewhere else or had something else to do, he would inform her. She waited until almost two and called. No answer.

She then drove over to the campus in her own car and found Bill's car in its usual place. She went to the chancellor's office, which is on the third floor of the Administration Building, and knocked and called his name but got no reply. She then went to the Student Center coffee shop and not seeing him there decided—feeling a little foolish, but by now a little worried—to call security and ask them to come and open his office to check. When the security man opened the door, they found his body on the floor not far from the door. The security man tried to resuscitate him, while Hannah called the hospital, but the body was already cooling and the security man soon gave up and called the police. The family physician, the ambulance, and the police all arrived at the same time, and Doc Jensen confirmed that he was dead. It was assumed that he had died of a heart attack or at least of natural causes since there were no signs of wounds or blood on the rug and the office door had been locked.

It was only after a routine autopsy that a bruise was discovered at the base of the skull that could not have been caused by his fall. In any case, he had been found lying face down. There had been little external bleeding, but massive injury to the brain. The police then searched the office and found a little matching blood on a piece of abstract bronze sculpture done by Matt Monroe of the university Art Department and given to the chancellor two years previously.

And that was it. The police, the sheriff, had certainly not announced they had anything beyond those facts, though they had questioned a number of people. If they did have any ideas, they were not saying, and the questions they had asked Hannah were mostly about the Trains' life before they arrived in Silvertown some fifteen years ago. Hannah had said they seemed to be searching for someone that Bill might have known in the past and asking about how happy their married life had been. If they were asking Hannah about her life with Bill, they didn't have much else to go on, because it was plain that they had been fond of each other and that they had worked well together in the chancellor's job. Bill had remarked on many occasions that Hannah did more than half his job and that he couldn't have lasted were it not for her.

It could be someone from the past, I thought, and if that were so, I wouldn't be able to discover very much. On the other hand, if it were someone from the university or the town, I might pick up some leads.

I worked somewhat absentmindedly through the morning on a land boundary problem. My client felt his neigh-

7

bor was appropriating several feet of his cornfield by placing his fence several feet beyond where he was sure the line was. (Bad neighbors make bad fences.) I drew up a suit against an insurance company offering another client less than the coverage called for after a farm vehicle accident, implying negligence. I never tried to bargain with that particular company, because they always tried to pay less; so I always sued them before I argued with them. I figured eventually the costs of being sued might persuade them to pay the full amount without ado whenever they discovered a client had me for his attorney.

But my mind was on Bill Train and the circumstances of his death. I decided by noon to begin my stab at the case by making sure of the known details. I called Harry Hansen, head of security at the university, and got the name of Jim Fountain, the man who had opened the door for Hannah. Jim was on his day off, and I reached him at home. He was working on his boat in the garage out back, and I could come and talk to him, though he had told what little he knew to the police.

I walked home for lunch and got my car. I had told Harry and Jim as well that I was trying to clear up some details for Hannah.

Short, stocky, about thirty, Jim was scraping old paint from his boat. He nodded his hunting cap at me to acknowledge my presence and went on scraping.

"Getting ready for the fishing season?" I said, friendly-like.

He nodded again.

"I'm sorry to bother you on your day off," I said. "But it would be helpful to Mrs. Train if you could go through your story again with me."

Jim shrugged. "O.K.," he said. "Nothing much in it." He put down the paint scraper and wiped his nose with his sleeve. Spring is mostly a cold season in northern Wisconsin, and I pulled my car coat tighter around me and buttoned it.

"I got this call from Mrs. Train. I was the only one in the office, so I locked up and drove to the Admin Building and met her just outside. We walked upstairs together. The elevator was out of order, which it is a lot of the time—though Mrs. Train said it was working when she went up the first time—and when we got to the chancellor's office, I knocked and Mrs. Train called 'Bill' a couple of times. I unlocked the door, and we went in, and there was the chancellor laying on the floor. I tried to resuscitate him, but he was already cooling, and I knew it was too late. She called Doc Jensen at the hospital, and then I called the police, and Jensen came with the others and said he was dead. And that's all I know." He wiped his nose again.

"But the door was locked?"

"Yeah, but it's one of those locks that can be set from the inside when you go out, you know, you push a button in and then just pull the door shut."

"So someone could have been inside with the chancellor and killed him and then locked the door as he went out."

"That's right. It must have been that way."

"And you can get into the Administration Building at any time?"

"No, it's locked at four on Saturday for the weekend."

"Did you notice anything unusual in the office?"

"What do you mean?"

"Anything that you wouldn't expect and hadn't seen before?"

"Well, I wouldn't know, because I've only been in his office once, when the committee went to see him."

"What committee was that?"

Jim shrugged. "We had a committee of the security personnel. We went to ask him to let us carry guns."

"Guns?"

9

"Yeah, we figured if we was in uniform and if anybody did come on campus and see the uniform they might try to use guns on us, and there we'd be."

"What did the chancellor say?"

Jim sniffed. "He said no. He said he didn't want any students getting hurt by accident. And if outsiders came on campus, we should call the Silvertown Police Department."

"I guess you weren't happy with that decision."

Jim shrugged again. "Professors and academic types sometimes don't know what the score is, but that's the way it is."

"I guess you didn't like Train very much then."

Jim looked up at me sharply. "He was all right otherwise, as far as I know."

"Were there people on the campus who didn't like him?"

"Sure. There was some students mad at him two years ago when he canceled that outdoor beer bust after he discovered they had been serving minors at the one before that."

"Did they talk of getting even?"

"Naw, they cooled down. Students thought he was fair on the whole."

"What about faculty?" The cold was getting to me. I blew on my hands.

"I never heard any professors saying anything. They mostly liked him, I think. Course there was Jim Pickel, the football coach, I guess he was mad as hell at the chancellor when he fired him from being coach." Jim grinned. "I thought he had it coming, but a lot of people thought Pickel was great stuff."

"Do you think Pickel could kill somebody?"

Jim pondered a moment. "Don't know. Maybe. But I'll tell you something, his wife could. She's something else."

I laughed. Maud Pickel is a tall, fierce woman with iron-gray hair who bosses her husband around like a shrew. Pickel, short, fat, and bald, was known as the meanest, cussingest coach in the state football league. His players worshipped him, but that didn't stop him from meekly following Maud's orders. He had been a show, whether he was a snorting little bull on the field, or Maud's mild little dachshund off.

I didn't know why he had been relieved of his coaching duties. Bill hadn't made any public statements or any private ones that I had heard, for that matter, about why he did it. Silvertown's football record had not been the greatest; we usually finished in the bottom half. My senior year the only team we beat was Platteville. Well, something there I should ask Hannah about. I knew Bill talked to Hannah about everything, she being the only one he could talk to with a guarantee of confidence.

"So you didn't notice anything out of the ordinary in the chancellor's office? Other than a dead body, that is."

Jim sniggered a little. Then he took on a serious look. "It's probably nothing. I mean I don't know how administrators work, but there's a conference table in that office, and I noticed the papers on it was scattered all over like somebody messed them up on purpose. Some even on the floor."

"What kind of papers?"

"I don't know. Just papers."

"With writing on them, typescript, computer printouts, what sort?"

"Well, it wasn't computer printouts, that much I know. Like typing sheets, that sort of thing."

"Scattered all over."

"Yeah. Mostly at one end of the conference table but really messy."

"Did you tell the police about the papers?"

"No, they didn't ask. Anyway, maybe that's the way the chancellor worked." He wiped his nose on his sleeve.

"Thanks, Jim. You've been helpful, and I know Mrs. Train will appreciate it." I shook his hand, and he nodded and went back to his scraping, as I drove back to my office with the heater on full blast.

# III

Once in my office I answered a few phone calls from clients, then called Harry Hansen again. I was making a kind of list in my mind of things I knew and didn't know and wanted to know.

"Harry," I said. "This is Sean Fogarty again. This Fountain guy mentioned a committee to see Train to ask permission to carry guns. What was that all about?"

Harry sighed. "Yeah, well, some of the young types we have on the security force here wanted to tote guns like real cops. I had mixed feelings about it, but the chancellor was opposed to it because he said the only kind of violence we were likely to have would be student protests against something or another, and he didn't want any lethal weapons on campus." Harry snorted. "I guess he never thought about modern sculpture as being lethal. Anyway, its too bad Fountain was on the committee—he was the most gung ho of the group for guns."

"Why was that too bad?"

"Well, we kept it quiet around here, but Fountain was on the police force in Beloit and killed a black in a raid on a gambling joint. He was exonerated, but of course he was no longer persona grata in Beloit. Train wasn't too happy when we hired Fountain—that was about three years ago—

13

and he was not about to let someone he suspected of being gun-happy have one."

"Do you think he's stable?" I said.

"Do I think he'd murder the chancellor? Is that what you're asking?" Harry barked a short laugh. "No. He's a little gung ho, like I said. He gives more parking tickets than anybody else, for not having a permit or to students for being in faculty slots, but he's not the murdering type."

"Of course, he is a killer," I pointed out.

"I can't deny that, but that was not being cool and probably scared and prejudiced. But not being allowed to carry a gun sure isn't enough reason for him to bash the chancellor's head in. Besides, the chancellor was white."

I thanked Harry and rang off. Being white is no comfort when you are dead, I thought, even if you're biased. I started to write down what I had learned from Fountain. The little item about the elevator needed to be cleared up. Fountain said the elevator in the Administration Building was usually out of order, but the point was it was in order, then out of order, that Saturday. I called Leif Ericson, who is head of maintenance on the campus. Leif's son and my daughter Cathy were classmates in high school, and I guess fairly good friends, until she went off to Connecticut College (she insisted on going east to college).

"What can I do for you, Counselor?" he said in his usual thin, nasal tone.

"Leif, I'm trying to help Hannah Train find out all she can about the circumstances of Bill's death. I don't know what good it will do, but anyway I'm going over some of the details, and I have a couple of questions."

"Yeah, that was bad. Train was a good man. What do you want to know?"

"I understand the elevator was out of order that Saturday."

"The cops asked me about that, too. It wasn't. It was

14

turned off and stuck in the basement. It has one of those buttons you can use to keep the doors open while you load it, supplies and stuff. The janitors use it—there's no freight elevator in that building. The cleaning crew found it there in the basement with the doors open on Monday morning."

"What did the cops make of that?"

"Nothing they told me about. You think the killer rode the elevator to the basement and left it open?"

"I don't know."

"Why would he do that?"

"I can't think of any reason," I said. "It just struck me as strange that it worked when Mrs. Train went up the first time then it wasn't working the next time. How about the exit from the basement?"

"Well, you'd have to climb a flight of stairs to go out the front, but you can go out the back on the same level. The building is on a slope."

"Would you be less likely to be noticed if you went out the back?"

"Yeah, I guess so, especially by people in the front." It's hard to know when Norwegians are being funny.

"Would it be less likely there would be somebody in the back to notice?" I said, after we laughed.

"I'd say so," Leif said, "if you was talking about Saturday, because the back faces Kinkaid Hall, which is a faculty office building. You don't often find faculty there on Saturday. On the other hand, the front of the building faces the mall, and there's always people on the mall if the weather isn't bad. Maybe you're right, maybe the killer did go out the back after fixing the elevator so nobody else could use it. But why would he want to stop the elevator?"

"Maybe had had something to haul out," I said.

"By damn, maybe you're right. Was something taken from the chancellor's office?"

"Good question," I said.

I put in a call to Doc Jensen. Doc Jensen had presided over the birth of our daughter, and his father, "Ole" Doc Jensen, had delivered me, so that to say Jensen is our family doctor is putting it mildly. More to the point, he was the chancellor's family physician and had been the first to examine Bill after Fountain had tried to bring back the dead by pushing and pulling on his chest. Jensen was with a patient, but his nurse said she would have him call back between this patient and the next.

I called the chancellor's secretary and gave her my helping-Hannah pitch. She seemed uneager to be of help, but agreed she would talk to me after two-thirty, when the acting chancellor planned to leave for Madison. The acting chancellor was the dean of instruction, the one I mentioned earlier as being the pal of a small group of fervent followers. His temporary appointment was seen by his friends as his chance to prove he should be Bill's successor. Faculty not in his coterie were not so keen about that prospect, according to my sources. Had he bludgeoned Bill to get his chance, I wondered? Unlikely. Bill would never have turned his back on him.

I sipped a cup of office coffee and made a face. Julie was a dear sweet soul, the model of secretarial efficiency, and she had been with me forever, but she couldn't make coffee. Susie suggested that perhaps she was trying to give me a message, but I pointed out that she had made bad coffee long before Women's Lib. Doc Jensen's call rescued me.

I gave him my pitch and asked him if he could pinpoint the time of death.

"Sometime between noon and two o'clock," Jensen said.

I was surprised. "But I thought Fountain had said the body was cooling."

"I understand that it was about two-thirty when Fountain finally let them into the office," Jensen said. "In any case, that's my guess, and it is borne out by the autopsy report."

"My God, that means the murderer could have been in the building when Hannah first knocked on the door."

"I suppose that's true, he or she could have been."

"Or she?"

"You don't think a woman could have done it?"

"That's really a question I should ask you," I said. "Wasn't that sculpture a little heavy for a woman to wield?"

"You have old-fashioned ideas about women," Jensen said. "I know women who could lift you above their heads, twirl you around, and toss you into a heap. Anyway, no, the sculpture as I remember it does not weigh more than what a reasonably strong woman could handle as a weapon."

"And that was definitely Bill's blood on the sculpture?"

"The blood type matches."

"It could have been someone's blood of the same type?"

"Highly unlikely. Possibly, of course, but I understand the police found matching hairs as well."

"Was there anything else of interest in the autopsy?"

"Nothing. The usual signs of being his age."

"Was he is good health?"

"Generally, yes. Not enough exercise, a little over-weight, a little arthritis."

"I noticed that he was slow getting up sometimes, and he seemed to favor his left side when he walked. I suppose that was arthritis."

"Possibly. Though you know he had been wounded badly in the war. He had a lot of scar tissue on his abdomen and the left back." Jensen never used technical language on the laity.

I was surprised again. "I didn't know anything about that. He never said anything about being a veteran. World War II?"

"I supposed so, given his age. Maybe the Korean War. I don't really know. He just told me he had been wounded in the war. That was the first time I examined him. I think he was sometimes in pain from it, but he didn't like to take pills, especially pain pills."

"What kind of wounds were they?"

"I'm not sure. Looked like shrapnel, lots of perforations."

"Could it have been something else, a knife, for example?"

"Why do you ask?"

"I just wondered."

"Could have been a knife, I suppose, if he were stabbed a number of times. There were a few old burn marks, too, and that suggests hot metal like shrapnel. What has all this to do with his murder?"

"I don't really know," I said. "Maybe something happened a long time ago that came back to take its—his—revenge. Or hers."

Jensen asked after Susie and Cathy, I thanked him, and we hung up.

Funny, even after being a lawyer for all these years, I keep being surprised by how much we don't know about our friends and neighbors.

# IV

Silvertown just sort of grew, like that character in Harriet Beecher Stowe's famous novel. Our streets appear to have been laid out by an intoxicated logger driving home late at night through a blinding snowstorm. In the hyped language of our tourist brochures—after proper attention has been drawn to our pristine lakes and primeval forests, the hunting and fishing therein and the splendid resorts thereon and therein—the town's eccentric lack of rational design is depicted as "uniquely charming." The map on the back of the brochure, showing how to get to the university, or various motels, or even how to get out of town once you have succeeded in penetrating it, is a cartographer's nightmare. Visitors tend to see every bit of our unique charm before they can find their way anywhere at all. The volunteer fire department carries a compass on its dashboard.

The University of Wisconsin—Silvertown also just grew. If eclectic is a style, then hectic is its further refinement, descriptive in the fullest measure of the miscellany of buildings, surpassingly handsome and grimly ugly that now march down the mall with the monotonous uniformity of state prisons, or now cluster in scenic clumps of pine.

The university started as a teachers training school in one square building that looks like the turn-of-the-century high school it was. The building still remains, an atrocious

19

piece of architecture, a tribute to the determination of sentimental alumni. As a member of the Alumni Association Board, I know them well. And of course teacher training was and is at the bottom of the list of educational priorities in the state. The university in Madison got the money, and the training of teachers in the boondocks was done in barns and, alas again, by other secondary and primary teachers turned professors. Silvertown grew, along with other teachers colleges, offering other kinds of courses— even arts and sciences, to provide some content for teaching. Then this and that got added, and they became state colleges and, finally, under our famous Governor Lucey, became units of the university system. The merger was supposed to level things out and at the same time save money. It did neither, of course.

The faculty in the former state colleges wanted the same salaries as their now colleagues at Madison and were sour about not getting them. Madison was mad about the dilution of support and prestige for the "Mother Ship." Keeping the faculty happy on any campus is a difficult job for a chancellor, especially campuses without distinction. Who wants to be undistinguished at an undistinguished institution?

Well, I was happy with dear old Silvertown—not sentimental, just happy that I'd gone there. I liked the place, its friendly faculty (and some were pretty good, having come to Silvertown for the hunting and fishing and less stressful life and not because it had or didn't have a "reputation"). Walking now in the cold spring across the mall, mingling with students in their jeans and windbreakers, I remembered my own student days with just a little bit of nostalgia. It happened to me every time I came on campus.

My nostalgia always ended when I came in sight of the Administration Building, the ugliest thing on the campus, uglier even than old Main. It was once the Art Building, before the new one was built and it was converted. They added a fancy new front with ramps for the handicapped and an elevator. Even the bricks don't match. The building looks like a Volkswagon Beetle with a Rolls-Royce radiator grille.

I rode the elevator (it was working) up to the third floor and sat myself down at the side of Betty Olson's desk, while she informed a caller that Acting Chancellor Hartpence had just left for Madison. She replaced the phone on its cradle and gazed at me apprehensively.

Bill had had a hard time finding good secretaries. He had gone through five or six in fifteen years. Either they were pretty and could type and be pleasant, and did not understand anything about the university, or they understood the university, snarled on the phone, and typed as badly as he did himself. The first one he had, inherited from his predecessor, was of the latter kind. He foisted her off on some hapless department that had no choice but to take her. Her husband had taken umbrage and threatened to sue. (Had they finally taken their revenge?) Betty Olson was the latest, old enough to be his mother, though I gather neither would have been likely to claim the other.

"I appreciate your willingness to talk with me," I began, fairly sure from her transparent alarm that her willingness was somewhat thin. Her hair was bleached a pale orange color, like the bleak light before a winter sunset. It was hard to take my eyes off it.

"Yes," she said.

"Was Chancellor Train neat in the way he kept his papers on his desk, or were things a bit messy as they are on mine?"

Betty looked surprised at the question, and perhaps offended for Bill. "Why, neat," she said. "He had a small stack of papers he was working on at the side of his desk, and when he was through with them, they went into the out box."

"Did he ever work on the conference table? With his papers, I mean."

"Sometimes," she said.

"Would the papers sometimes get a little messy there?"

"Oh, no," she said, shaking her orange hair like a faded dustmop.

"I understand he worked on his own projects sometimes on Saturdays."

She had begun to grow calmer as the questioning began; now, however, the apprehension I had first noticed reappeared in the form of a frown. "I don't know very much about his own projects. He wrote articles and things. Sometimes I would do the final draft for him. He was a terrible typist."

"Was there anything secret or especially valuable about his articles or projects or whatever he worked on?"

She became rigid, as though something had protruded, uninvited, from her chair. "I wouldn't know about that."

"Do you know if he was working on a project at the time of his death?"

"I wouldn't know."

"You *wouldn't* know?"

"No."

"*Do* you know?" The lawyer in me was coming out. She shook her head.

"If he had a project going, didn't he leave some of his work on the conference table, or somewhere?"

"Oh, no. He always put his papers away when he was working on university things or meeting with people."

"Did he keep them in a special place?"

"In his file. Or he took them home."

"Was anything missing from the office when you returned on the Monday after his death?"

She shuddered. "The statue," she said.

"I suppose the police have that."

She nodded.

"Anything else?"

She seemed to think a minute, then she shook her head.

"Suppose I told you he had been working on a big project and that the papers were scattered over the conference table at the time he was killed."

She stared at me in alarm. "I don't know anything about that," she said in a small voice.

"What happened to those papers?"

"I don't know," she said. She began to twist a pencil in her hands. "I didn't see any papers when I got here on Monday."

Either she didn't know anything about the papers or she was stonewalling me. I decided to change the subject.

"Who would want to kill Chancellor Train?"

"I don't know. I don't know why anyone would do that." She seemed stricken. "The police asked me that, too."

"Had anybody come to see him recently who was angry?"

"I never saw any angry people in this office. Except Coach Pickel, and that was last year."

"You opened the chancellor's mail, didn't you?"

"Yes, except what was marked confidential."

"He got confidential letters?"

"Yes."

"From where?"

She shrugged. "I don't know, really. Madison and Washington sometimes. Even interoffice."

"Did you open any angry letters?"

"Well." She seemed to be trying to think. "There was a letter from Mr. Penney."

23

"Angry?"

"Yes."

"What about?"

"Because he was being shifted from his job in the registrar's office to the bursar's office."

"Why was he being shifted?"

"I don't know, but he didn't want to leave the registrar's office. The chancellor sent him a letter informing him that he was being transferred, and he objected. He said he'd been in the registrar's office for ten years and that he should have been promoted to registrar when that fell open last year and that the chancellor had no right to move him like that, and he was going to file a grievance with the Regents."

"Any others?"

"Last year there was that woman from Women's Studies who complained about the way women were being treated on the campus."

"Others?"

"There was Dr. Rector from the English Department. She was mad about the way the raise money was distributed, or something like that."

"I've heard she creates fusses about almost everything."

"She sure was in the office a lot about something or other."

"Was she always mad about something?"

"Well, she's always been nice to me, but I heard her voice getting loud in the chancellor's office."

"Anyone else?"

"A lot of people came to the see the chancellor, and I don't know whether they were angry or not. He never asked me to ask them in advance what they wanted, because he always said anybody could come to see him whenever they wanted to whenever he was here."

"He was away a lot?"

24

"He was in Madison a lot. I heard him tell a faculty committee once as they were leaving the office that his real job was getting things from Madison for Silvertown."

"Any other angry people?"

"Well, there was a batch of letters from alumni when Pickel was removed from his coaching job. One in particular I remember, because he said the chancellor wouldn't get away with it."

"Do you have that letter?"

"It's in the file."

"May I see it?"

"I don't know whether I should let you see stuff from the file. I'd have to ask Dr. Hartpence."

"Would you ask him for me, please? And let me know."

"Yes, sir."

"Anything you can think of that might tell us something about who murdered the chancellor, I'd appreciate your informing me. You should tell the police, too, of course. But I'm acting for Mrs. Train. O.K.?"

She nodded and looked relieved that I was standing up to go. That was the point I thought I'd better shake her up a little, since she'd not been forthcoming about the papers.

"Remember," I said, "that withholding information about a murder makes one an accessory after the fact."

She sat up straight. "Yes, sir," she said.

I thanked her politely.

# V

When I got home, Susie announced that she was taking me out to dinner at Jolly's. That meant, of course, that she didn't want to cook. Jolly's is *the* restaurant in Silvertown, owned, surprisingly enough, not by Nate Colby (though his bank provided financing), but by Peter Jolly. Jolly more than lives up to his name. He has an electronic grand piano that is connected to all sorts of bells and chimes and drums and bird whistles located over your head that will go off without warning as you eat. The distractions are sometimes useful, given the quality of the food. There is an infinite variety of the latter, listed in seventeen pages of menu, all frozen, except steaks and prime rib. Most of us locals order the beef, and the out-of-towners, who come to see and hear our native Liberace in his hand-decorated silk shirt, order the fancy dishes that are occasionally not all thawed out in the microwave. But the ambience is pleasant, and you see everybody you know there sometime during the week. We ordered our steaks and talked over our drinks, a glass of chablis for Susie, a Dewar's on the rocks for me.

I reported to Susie on my detective work for the day. I had completed the fact finding: the time of death (between twelve and two) and the physical circumstances (locked door, but easily locked by the departing guest; the elevator

26

on stop in the basement; the weight of the death weapon, wieldable by male or female; the possibility that the murderer might well have been seen by someone in the mall if he exited from the front of the building, or possibly not at all if he exited from the back). And I had uncovered what might be a bit of a mystery: the "messy" papers on the conference table not known about or discovered by the secretary (or she was covering up for some reason). And some suspects of a sort: Pickel, the fired coach; Fountain, the frustrated gunslinger; Rector, the troublemaker; the Women's Studies Department; an angry alumnus; a transferred assistant registrar. The list, Susie noted, was not very convincing and much too short. She was duly impressed by my basic information, however, and curious about the papers.

"What could they have been?" She mused, sipping her chablis, looking glamorous, at forty, in the dim light.

"Might simply have been an article on Plato," I said.

"But why would anyone remove and cover up a draft of an article on Plato?"

"Maybe it was an annual report on the quality of the Education Department."

"Don't be mean," she said.

"And why," she went on, "would Bill's secretary not open all his letters, even the ones marked confidential? What would be so confidential his personal secretary shouldn't see them?"

"Maybe he was getting love leters from an old flame, or maybe he's working for the CIA," I offered.

"Sean," she reproved me. "Bill wouldn't be getting love letters. He was a model of uprightness."

"Uprightness?"

"Behave yourself. You're in public. As for the CIA, what would they want with an agent in Silvertown? To spy on the Canadians?"

"By the way," I said, "she said letters that came confidential came from Madison and Washington. Confidential letters from Madison could be about personnel matters, I suppose. But Washington? Do we do secret research for the Pentagon here at Silvertown? Our science departments are scarcely that advanced."

"Whatever those papers were about, and whatever kind of confidential mail he got, you have to dig into it, that's for sure. Would Hannah know?"

The waitress brought our orders before we decided what the answer to that question was. Steaks, one rare and one well done (we are a disaster ordering a Wellington together), baked potatoes, salad, good old American Middle West food. The good old American Midwest, where we murder our chancellors, I thought, as we chewed.

"We haven't gotten far," I said, between bites.

"Nero Wolfe didn't solve any cases in an afternoon either," she comforted. She looked up. "Uh oh," she said through the side of her mouth, "here come de sheriff."

Sure enough, there was Bert Anderson, wearing his western-style stretch leisure suit, looming over us.

"How you doin', Bert," I said heartily.

"O.K., Counselor," said Bert. "How you doin'?"

"Just fine and dandy," I said. Susie kicked me under the table.

"I understand," he said, coming to the point with his usual finesse, "you been playin' sheriff."

"Who? Me?" I said, "I'm not smart enough to be a sheriff," I said. "I'm just a country lawyer."

Susie covered her face with her hands.

"I heard you say that before," the sheriff said. "What are you doin', messing in the chancellor's murder?"

"Well, I'll tell you Bert. In the first place, it's a free country, and in the second, Hannah Train has hired me, as you well know, to help her find out the circumstances

28

of her husband's unfortunate demise." (There I was, exaggerating again. At some point I'd better tell Hannah what I was doing, or she'd spoil my story.)

"The proper investigative agency, Counselor, is the Silvertown Police first of all and then the county sheriff. I can tell you that we have also the Criminal Investigation Bureau to help us, too. That ought to cover it, don't you think?" His face was a little red after that long speech.

"We all voted for you, Bert, and we have confidence in your ability to uncover the perpetrators of malfeasance in our county, but surely you don't begrudge my asking a few questions as well. The widow of the murdered man has a right to make inquiries or to ask her attorney to make inquiries. We can even hire a private detective, if we wish. We will certainly turn over any information pertinent to the case to the proper authorities."

"Fogarty," he said, his face even redder than it was before, "stay out of this. We don't want nobody messing up our investigation. Is that clear?"

"Are you threatening me, Sheriff?"

"No, sir, I'm just giving you some friendly advice." He lumbered off.

Susie rounded her lips into a big O.

"Wow," she said. "What was *that* all about?"

"Well," I said, "it could be he's still sore about that student marijuana case I beat him on because of the way he handled the evidence. Or . . ."

"Or?"

"Or he's truly touchy enough about someone else working on the case."

"Or?"

"Or there is more to this case than meets the eye."

"The papers?"

My steak was getting cold. "Could be," I said.

# VI

The following morning as I was shaving, I remembered I hadn't told Susie about Bill's scars, so I told her over breakfast. She was surprised, though she didn't know why Bill would want to mention it.

"I suppose Hannah knew," I said.

Susie laughed. "I would think so," she said.

"Unless Bill was like Grandma Keyes."

Susie laughed again. Grandma Keyes had informed Susie's mother as she was growing into her teens that her husband had never seen her in anything less than a slip. It was a family joke that a lot of things must have happened in the dark since Susie's mother had nine brothers and sisters.

"Bill never mentioned being in the war," Susie said. "And Hannah didn't."

"Bill was not the kind to talk about himself," I reminded her. "And the war was a long time ago."

It was Susie's opinion that I should talk with Dr. Jackson, who was president of the Faculty Senate. He would know about disgruntled faculty members. And I'd better talk to Hannah. She would ask Hannah to dinner. She had been meaning to do that anyway. I agreed and trotted off to my office at my usual brisk pace.

As I started to cross Main, I saw an ancient Nash turn

into Main from Seventh Street. I stepped back hurriedly. It was Minerva Hightower. Even though you couldn't see her face, because it was mostly below the dashboard, you knew. A big hat filled the space between the bottom of the steering wheel, where her ancient blue eyes peered over the dash, and the roof of the car. A cigarette dangled from her mouth. She drove down the middle of Main. Pedestrians rushed to the curbs. A Datsun pickup coming the other way mounted the sidewalk and removed from its pinions the last bench left from the Chamber of Commerce's beautification project. I watched, and miraculously, again she reached First Street without a single death and disappeared. Even the fire truck on its way to a fire was known to stop and let her go by, lest the city be faced with the expensive purchase of a new truck. Her successful passage (except for the unfortunate Datsun) was a happy harbinger for the day.

I had hardly gotten to my office and begun to go through my mail (Julie opens everything for me, even letters from old flames and instructions from the CIA), when a call came from Harold Hartpence, the acting chancellor. The phone sounded like long distance, and I remembered he had gone to Madison the afternoon before. Must be important, I thought, as we exchanged greetings.

Hartpence cleared his throat. I could visualize him, short and chubby, in his Moe (of the Three Stooges) haircut. "I understand," he said, "you want to look at some material in the chancellor's file."

I agreed that I did, and I went into my inquiring-for-Hannah routine.

"I don't want to obstruct your search, but we generally don't let outsiders read the private correspondence that comes to the university."

So he did want to obstruct my search. "I'm not interested in reading private correspondence that comes into the uni-

31

versity," I said. "I'm interested in doing what I can, at Mrs. Train's request, to uncover the facts surrounding Chancellor Train's murder. Mrs. Train is legally entitled to information of this sort." (I wasn't quite sure of my legal ground as to reading university files, but I thought I might as well throw the weight of the law around, since he was throwing the university's weight around.)

"Well, I will instruct Mrs. Olson to allow you to see the letter she mentioned to you, but that will have to be the end of it."

I had begun to get a funny feeling obstruction was the name of the game. Had Sheriff Anderson gotten to Acting Chancellor Hartpence?

"I appreciate your cooperation, Dr. Hartpence. I have no desire to rummage through your files, but I will have to follow through whatever trail of pertinent facts I turn up. Thank you again." I hung up.

I asked Julie to call Penney, Rector, the chairwoman of Women's Studies, whatever her name was, Pickel, Jackson, Chief James of the Silvertown Police Department, and the chief of the police department in Beloit, and went back to my morning mail.

Chief Dicky James of the Silvertown Police Department was the first one Julie reached. Dicky was an old timer, with shaggy white hair and a face full of ancient valleys, who knew almost before it happened who had stolen some tools from Fred Lily's pickup or who started the fight in Clancy's Tavern. He was good with high school kids when they were tempted to become delinquent, as I could testify from my own days in Silvertown High (but I'm not going into that). His wife had died of cancer the year before. His devotion to her during her illness had touched us all.

I told him what I was up to. Before I asked, he said he would help to the extent he could.

"The sheriff's in charge now. We sort of overlap, but we try to cooperate. He's been in contact with the state Criminal Investigation Bureau, too."

"Did you find any fingerprints on the sculpture or in the office?" I asked.

"A few. We found some prints of the chancellor and one of Len Garret, the janitor, on the top of the sculpture. The bottom where the killer must have held it had been wiped clean. A lot of prints on the conference table of the chancellor, Betty Olson, Hartpence, Yeats, some of the deans. They must have had a meeting there Friday, because the prints were mostly pretty clear and the table had not been waxed over as I gather it usually is. Looks like whoever did it was careful."

"Any physical evidence of any other kind?"

"Not that we can be sure of."

"Were there papers on the conference table?"

"Papers?" Dicky answered that one slowly. "What kind of papers?"

"Any kind of papers. Jim Fountain told me he saw a conference table full of messy papers when he and Hannah discovered the body."

"I don't know anything about papers," Dicky said.

"Come on, Dicky, you're hedging. Is there some special thing about those papers that you have been told not to talk about?"

"You'll have to ask the sheriff about that, Sean. I don't have nothin' to do with papers on the conference table."

"Has the sheriff put a lid on you? He tried to warn me off last night from looking into this case."

Dicky hesitated again. "Well, I guess he can't stop you from helping your client, can he. I wouldn't try to stop you, Sean. You know that. What the sheriff does, well, that's his business, I guess."

"Damn it, Dicky, you and I have been friends for a long time, and you've always been straight with me like an uncle. What is going on?"

"I still feel like an uncle to you, Sean. But I have to do what I have to do. And so do you, I guess. And anyway, I won't get in your way."

"You *are* in my way."

He didn't answer.

"Are there any suspects?"

"Not really. We're still working on it. It's fair to say we don't have any *proper* suspects."

"Is it an inside or outside job?"

"I really don't know. With what little we know, it could be either."

"All right, Dicky. I appreciate your help as far as you seem to be able to give it."

"Sean, if you uncover anything interesting, let me know, will you?"

"Tit for tat," I said and hung up.

# VII

The chief in Beloit was the second to come through. I identified myself and what I was up to. He remarked that the murder of the chancellor was really something, and what could he do to help? I told him I was interested in Jim Fountain, that probably he wouldn't be so bold as to murder a chancellor, but he did seem gun-happy.

"The chancellor called me about Fountain, you know. He asked about the case here where Fountain killed that black. I told him I thought Fountain would be all right if he didn't carry a gun. The chancellor said he didn't intend to let any of his security people carry guns. He said he was reluctant to hire Fountain anyway, but the chief of security and the assistant chancellor for administration had already promised him the job, so he supposed he would go ahead and approve it. I thought the chancellor was killed with a piece of sculpture."

"That's true, but I gather Fountain was pretty frustrated when he wasn't allowed to tote a gun. He organized a committee and requested permission to carry guns but got turned down. I suppose that's not really a motive for murder. I wondered just how violent Fountain could be, whether he is stable, whether he might use any weapon at hand if he were in a rage?"

The chief hesitated a moment. "I'm not really sure. Some

guys who want to be cops have a streak of violence in them. We try to weed out the ones that seem to have a personal stake in violence, but we don't always spot them. I guess I really can't be sure about Fountain. He resented authority. He specially didn't like me, after he killed that black man and I didn't stand up for him. I had to play that one real cool. It wasn't exactly a clean case." He seemed to be hesitating again.

"What do you mean?" I said.

"Well, I don't want anything on the record, and I didn't mention this to the chancellor when he called about Fountain. Maybe I should have, but it was a policeman's hunch."

"Okay," I said. "Nothing on the record."

"The shooting incident with Fountain involved drugs. The raid, in fact, was based on a tip Fountain said he got from an informer. It's possible Fountain killed this guy because of drugs."

"Fountain was running his own anti-drug operation?"

"That's one possible answer. Another is he was running a pro-drug operation. There's a big war going on here between two drug gangs, one white, one black, and the guy that bought it was a big dealer for the black gang. It just could be that Fountain did the killing for the white gang."

"Good God, you mean Fountain may have been an enforcer for a drug outfit?"

"I may be wrong, but what I do know is the killing was a service for the white outfit. Add to that the fact that we had been losing drugs taken in raids and being held as evidence, from our supposedly secure property room. And after Fountain left, we didn't lose any for a year. Pretty circumstantial, maybe just coincidental, I grant, but an interesting set of circumstances at least."

"So the university here has a possible drug enforcer on its security staff?"

"Bad, I know, but I didn't know about the stolen drugs—and the destruction of evidence—when the chancellor called me for a reference on Fountain. You have to be careful about blackballing somebody these days anyway, you know. They sue. Damned lawyers. Sorry about that, Counselor."

I winced. "I understand," I said. "And I thank you very much for your help."

"Good luck."

Now there was a suspect of the first water. Bill Train discovers one of his campus cops (the one who wants to carry a gun) is a drug enforcer and orders him to quit or he'll fire him, and campus cop takes him out with an objet d'art. And then campus cop helps discover body and even essays to resuscitate same. But what about the messy papers Fountain had told me about? A made-up story? A red herring?

Julie reached Pickel for me next, but after I explained what it was I wanted to talk to him about, Pickel got huffy and said he would not talk to me except in the presence of his attorney. I said I was not a policeman, but he repeated he wouldn't talk to me without his attorney. And hung up. That was a bust.

Five minutes later Gary Heiser of Crowe, Denison and Heiser called.

"Sean," he said.

"Gary," I said. "How are things?"

"Real good, Sean. Say, listen, Coach Pickel just called me and said you wanted to talk to him about the chancellor's murder."

"Yes," I said. "That's right. Hannah Train has retained me, and I'm looking into the case."

"Why do you want to talk to Pickel?"

"Well, I understand a lot of old phys ed alumni were angry when the chancellor asked Pickel to step down from coaching and go back to teaching. I even remember a lot of illiterate letters to the editor of the *Silvertown Bee*. I thought maybe Pickel would know if any one of them might have been mad enough to get back at Train."

"Well, Pickel doesn't want to talk to you. I have advised him that he doesn't have to."

"That's not very helpful, Gary. I realize he didn't exactly appreciate the chancellor after he had to step down, but surely he doesn't want to see a murderer go free. And doesn't that make Pickel look a little strange?"

"The police are looking into the murder, Sean. We'll just let them handle it, and if they want to talk to Pickel, why maybe he will, with me present. Sorry."

"I'm sorry, too, Gary," I said and hung up.

"Well," I said aloud to myself, "that's a pretty pickle."

Julie was just entering my office with some papers and made a face like she was drinking some of her own coffee.

Penney was next, and not exactly friendly, but he would see me in the bursar's office whenever. Then Jackson said he would talk to me anytime after his last class, which was over at two. Rector, sounding hoarse and brittle, said she would see me at three. Nobody was answering at the Women's Studies office.

I busied myself with the law the rest of the morning, went home to lunch at noon. Susie had canned salmon salad on Ritz with peperoncinis on the side waiting for me. I drove over to the university a little after one and parked in the faculty parking area. We members of the Alumni Association Board have special stickers on our windshields. I hoped that would protect me from Officer Fountain.

Penney looks like Richard Nixon. His five-o'clock shadow is full grown by one-forty-five. His eyes keep shifting so much when you talk to him, you wonder if he's watching a tennis game over your shoulder. He agreed at once that he hadn't liked the chancellor because he had been treated unfairly. He was in line to be promoted to registrar when the incumbent retired, and instead the chancellor gave the job to a lady faculty member. Six months later he had been shifted to the bursar's office. He had no complaints about the bursar's office, and he had not lost any salary, but clearly his self-esteem had been injured. And clearly he had a lot to injure. But he resented any implication that his resentment at being treated unfairly might have induced him to murder the chancellor.

"I suppose," I said, "there are other people who were not that keen about the chancellor."

"You bet," he said.

"Who are they?"

His eyes alternated between my left shoulder and my right shoulder and then down at his desk. He was thinking. "Hank Green in the Biology Department," he said finally.

"Why didn't he like the chancellor."

"Because of Pickel. Hank worked for Pickel at the stadium. And because Train wouldn't promote him. He is still an assistant professor after twenty years of service to Silvertown."

"Why hasn't he been promoted?"

"That's the question," Penney sneered. He looked even more like Nixon.

"Does Green have a Ph.D.?"

"No, but when he came to Silvertown, it wasn't required. Other faculty have been promoted over the years without Ph.D.s, and anyway, what's that got to do with good teaching?"

"Is Green a good teacher?"

Penney shrugged. "Sure."

"Were many faculty without Ph.D.s promoted after Train arrived?"

"Not many, all right. Train thought everybody should have the Ph.D."

"Do you think he would be angry enough about not getting promoted to murder the chancellor?"

Penney laughed dourly. "No, I don't think Hank would do that, but the morale of some people on this campus is so low that it could happen."

"It did happen that the chancellor was murdered," I pointed out.

"It could have been an insider that was mad at him."

"How about you?"

As they flickered wildly, his eyes actually met mine for a fraction of a second. "You don't have any right to say something like that to me. I was in Madison all that day. I have witnesses."

"Nobody has a right to murder the chancellor, whatever his feelings about his personnel decisions," I said.

He looked really sour.

"And you have witnesses that you were in Madison?"

"Yeah. A whole slew of relatives." He sneered.

"Anybody else besides Green who might have wanted to do the chancellor in?" I said.

He shook his head. "I don't know," he said.

I thanked him.

Hank Green was too dumb to have murdered the chancellor and not been caught in the act. His extracurricular job of playing janitor at the stadium was exactly right for him. Or was I taking him too lightly? Dumb people sometimes get very clever when they avenge themselves for their shortcomings.

As I walked out into the corridor, I heard a shout behind me. It was Rusty Yeats, assistant chancellor for administration. He was waving at me to come on down to his office. Rusty is a fellow Irishman and a good man besides. He has seven daughters, wears something green at all times. Even his golf cart is green. Bill Train had remarked to me on more than one occasion that Rusty was the best staff person he had at Silvertown. It is hard to find an administrative type, he said, who understands that a university is run for its students and faculty and not necessarily for efficiency in accounting.

"What are you doing over here in enemy territory?" Rusty said.

We had kidded each other in the past about town-gown relationships. I explained my mission, and he got solemn. Bill had been a good friend as well as his boss. Rusty shook his head. "I simply can't accept it that he's dead. And especially the way he died. It's beyond understanding." I remembered how shaken Rusty had looked at the funeral.

"But it did happen," I said.

"You were talking to Penney, I'll bet."

"Yes, I was. I understand he had a grievance."

Rusty shook his head, his long rusty hair falling over his eyes. He brushed it away. Rusty is tall and angular. He seems to have been put together by plumbers, with pipes for bones and tees and wyes for joints, and no curves. "Penney hasn't got the guts to do anything like that," he said. "He's snide and mean, but no hero."

"He gave me Green's name as a possibility."

"His good friend Green." He laughed. "They're two of a kind, except Green is even less a hero."

"But there are disgruntled staff and faculty here and there, aren't there?"

"Oh, sure. There has to be. And there are. Bill made a lot of tough decisions. He used to say every time you make a decision, somebody doesn't like it. And after fifteen years, that adds up. Of course some people recover from being passed over for tenure or promotion one year if they get it in another. And most people, I think, recognized that he had to make the decisions. Of course some egos are never assuaged, no matter how right the decisions. Ego is more important than logic."

"Betty Olson said he spent a lot of time in Madison."

"Fair amount. But, of course, that's where the money comes from and the buildings, not from the Silvertown Kiwanis Club. The Regents liked him. He was somebody in his own right, not an administrative hack. In the beginning, they were surprised he would come to Silvertown. Then they began to see Silvertown through his eyes. When they thought of Silvertown, they thought of Bill Train. He never asked for impossible things. He always made his case, and he got what he asked for because they respected him and had confidence in his judgment. That didn't come about because he went to the Silvertown Bowling Alley every Saturday night."

"Did he have any special friends in Madison?"

"Special friends? What do you mean?" Rusty was puzzled and a little suspicious.

"Special. Lady friends, for example."

"Holy Mary, Sean, what kind of question is that?"

"One I have to ask, if I'm going to cover all the possibilities."

"Well, I certainly don't know of any. And I don't believe there were any. He wasn't the bottom-pinching type. Anyway, what would that have to do with his murder?"

"The French have a saying."

"He wasn't French. And he was almost sixty years old." Rusty was offended.

"Some old types never give up."

Rusty laughed. "You're casting your fly against the wind."

"What type was he?"

"Well, you knew him. I worked for him for fifteen years. You get to know someone pretty well in that time. He was straight. He could operate when he had to. A little aloof, maybe. He could be pretty succinct. He was friendly, but no back slapper. I take that back. I did see him slap some backs in Madison. To see him work there was to see

42

another side. He adapted himself to the person he needed to influence, but even then he never gave away what he was. Never condescended. I think that may have cost him something, because he was an intellectual, Eastern type, and Silvertown ain't Boston. He was not of the Silvertown Chamber ilk. That may have been a lack in some eyes. When he had to cater, he did it with grace. I guess that sounds like a contradiction."

"Did he have a temper?"

"He sure as hell did. He'd shake his shaggy head and get mad. But he could control it when he needed to."

"Did he get mad at anybody in particular?"

"He was always particular, but he never treated anybody unfairly. He'd cool down. His anger was always justified, in my opinion, but it didn't get in the way of making good decisions in the end."

"Who'd he get angry at?"

"Faculty members who screwed things up. He believed in shared governance, even more than some faculty did. But that meant the faculty had to make responsible recommendations. Some of them didn't want to do that. He'd send the recommendations back for reconsideration. He protected good faculty members from their peers. A lot of them didn't know how he operated in Madison for their benefit either. He didn't make a big noise about it. Funny thing, he really didn't like praise. He'd praise others, but he couldn't stand it himself. He was just doing his job. If we got a bigger budget allocation than we had a right to expect, or a new building, that was simply his job."

"Can you remember a particular person he got mad at?"

"He got mad at Pickel."

"Why?"

"He gave Pickel a terrific deal to step down—voluntarily, as it were. A light teaching load, one of the highest salaries in the university. Pickel accepted the deal, then he went to the alumni athletic types and groused. Probably Maud made him do it. I think Bill was sorry he made such a good deal for him. He was mad at Pickel for lying to the press about it, but then he began to feel sorry for him, telling the public he had been fired when he could have retired from coaching gracefully."

"Why did Bill ask him to step down?"

"There were several reasons. Basically, because we felt that it was time for a change. He'd been football coach for several decades, and we wanted new leadership there. But there were concrete problems, a kind of cavalier attitude toward the assistant coaches, a feeling that he thought he owned the stadium. And, confidentially, a little problem with accountability that could have been embarassing had it become public."

"What was that?"

"Let's just say it was financial management, and that Pickel wouldn't cooperate with us to get it straightened out. Coaches, God knows, get that way often enough. They are above chancellors and the rest of the university. Sometimes that's borne out in their salaries in major universities. With the help of the jock-sniffer alumni, they thumb their noses at administrators and go their own way. Train was not about to let anybody do anything like that to Silvertown."

"Could Pickel have been mad enough to murder Train in revenge?"

"Maybe. Maud Pickel could."

I laughed. I'd heard that one before. "What about some ex-jock alumnus? There were all those illiterate letters in the *Silvertown Bee* attacking Train."

"I suppose that's possible, too. It comes from their training in good sportsmanship." He laughed. "In all honesty, though, I don't think we can accuse Pickel of training his footballers in sportsmanship."

"Can you think of anybody else sore enough—and hero enough, as you put it—to have done it?"

"I really can't. I've thought about it, believe me. But it has to have been somebody from off campus."

"Any students sore enough?"

Rusty thought a minute. "There was one student. He was black. He was dropped for academic reasons. He'd been dropped several times, and he wouldn't take any help from the Multicultural Center, where we have tutoring and where a lot of minorities go for special help. He appealed to the Standards Committee, and they turned him down—they had readmitted him twice. And finally he went to the chancellor, who, after looking at the record and the number of chances we had already given him, turned him down, too. The student was pretty angry, claiming racial discrimination. He asked Bill if he wasn't afraid of being assassinated like John Kennedy and Martin Luther King. The chancellor said he was too busy to think about it, and, besides, he wasn't important enough to be assassinated. Ironic, huh? Bill told me about the threat with his little wry smile. But he was unhappy about having to turn the kid down. The other black students who knew this kid were mad at him, for making a big fuss when he deserved what he got."

"Think he could have done it?"

"I don't know. I didn't know the kid, though he was arrogant enough the time he came to the Standards Committee."

"What was his name?"

"I can't remember. I'll get it for you."

"Anybody else?"

He laughed. "Rector?"

"Rector?"

"I don't think so. She was a pain in Bill's side, in all our sides, if not some other section of the anatomy. She's certainly big enough, but I think it would be against her principles to do something herself. She always made the big noise and then let somebody carry the ball for her causes."

"I'm supposed to see her at three this afternoon," I said.

He grinned. "Take your shillelagh along."

# VIII

Dr. Jackson was standing outside his office talking to a small group of students, apparently about the latest exam he had just returned. Various odors from the chemistry labs assaulted my nostrils. Jackson waved me on into the physics office and continued for a moment to explain a point the students were having difficulty grasping. Jackson looks like a small version of the early (sans beard), homely Abraham Lincoln, and has a slow and deliberate manner. Bill had respected him, I knew, and Jackson reciprocated. He has been elected president of the Faculty Senate off and on over his long tenure at the university, and that surely suggests he also has the respect of his fellow professors.

"Mr. Fogarty," he said, "please sit down." He waved me to a chair beside his desk. "Students seem to listen more carefully after they have missed something on an exam, and don't know why, than they do when you first explain it to them. You would think they were more interested in exams and grades than in learning. What can I do for you?"

I gave him my pitch.

His eyes clouded up. "A terrible thing," he said. "It's still hard to believe."

"Are there faculty members who might feel they had grievance enough to do something like that?"

"I've thought about that," he said slowly. "Maybe one or two, but feeling like doing it and doing it are two different things."

"Who might feel that way?"

"Wilbur Richards, maybe."

"I guess I don't know him," I said.

"He's in sociology. Enrollment has been falling in sociology for some time, and this last year they were told they would have to cut one position. The position would have to go to computer science, which has been growing rapidly. The department was informed by the chancellor that the Executive Committee had made that decision, but the Sociology Department would have to decide which untenured person would not be reappointed. They had a hard time deciding because they didn't want to grow smaller, but after considering who was essential to the program in terms of expertise and teaching and who was not, they chose Richards."

"And?"

"It turns out Richards is part American Indian."

"So he claimed discrimination."

"Right. Well, the department has a black woman and an Hispanic, which is more minorities than any other department in Arts and Sciences has, but that was his claim. He sued the university, the chancellor, the dean, the department, and Board of Regents."

"What happened to the suit?"

"He lost, but that didn't stop him."

"What else did he do?"

"He organized some sympathetic people here and brought in some Indians from the reservation. I don't know what his tribe is—he's only a quarter Indian anyway, and he doesn't look Indian, but I guess that's enough. There was a sit-in in the chancellor's office, a lot of hot words, and some threats."

I remembered, then, the little sit-in. It hadn't lasted long. I hadn't known that threats had been made. Bill hadn't said very much about it. Hannah had told Susie, and Susie told me.

"Richards is still on campus?"

"Yes. His appointment is up at the end of the spring term."

"Do you think he is capable of murder?"

"I just don't know," he said slowly. "Somebody is, and I guess you have to look at motive. I've been thinking about it, as I said, and he is the one that came to mind." He leaned back in his chair and looked out the window. "I think he's a little crazy, too."

"How do you mean?"

"Just that he's sometimes incoherent. At least I couldn't understand him when he came to the senate and made the argument that we should impeach the dean, the chancellor, and the chairman of Sociology."

"Impeach?" I laughed. "Well, that's a new one."

"Shared governance carried to its logical extreme," he said. "Anyway, he said a lot of wild things in that meeting, and we finally had to ask him to keep quiet or leave."

"And he left."

"And he left. I haven't heard anything in the last month or so. He has applied for other positions, I heard, but he isn't talking about whether he has one yet or not. Sociology isn't the hottest field right now. Though of course with affirmative action and all that sort of thing, somebody ought to bite."

"Who knows him well that would talk to me about him?"

He pondered for a minute. "Dick Wright. He's chairman of Sociology and was his friend until the big blowup."

"Anybody else who might be capable of murder?"

"There was Nelson, who was removed from being dean

of business. He was pretty unhappy about it and said a lot of nasty things about the chancellor to his colleagues in accounting, to which he had to return, but I doubt . . . And I don't know whether I should say anything about this one or not, but I guess the interests of justice supercede those of privacy. Two years ago the chancellor fired a tenured faculty member for sexual harassment. Or rather he told him he would set up a committee to hear the charges or grant a sabbatical with pay upon receiving a resignation."

That one I had heard nothing about at all.

"The chancellor consulted just three of us on the faculty about it and swore us to secrecy. He was taking full responsibility, but he wanted to be sure to have representative faculty opinion. That was Steve Wallace in Mathematics. The case against him was pretty strong, and the chancellor showed him the evidence upon which the hearing would be based. Wallace took the sabbatical. His resignation takes effect this June."

"Well, I'll be damned," I said. "Do you think Wallace could have done it?"

"I don't know. He was pretty good at intimidating women students, I guess, but I don't know whether he could commit murder. He was surely desperate, especially since he had a wife and five kids. Murder would not be a way to solve his problem, but he may have thought his life was in ruins."

"Did he get another job?"

"I don't know."

"Is he still in town?"

"I think so. And while I'm revealing confidential matters, there was one more case of student complaints against a faculty member, this time for drunkeness in class. A group of students claimed that they had observed him drunk on the campus and downtown and that they had smelled liquor on his breath frequently in class. They said his conduct was irrational on occasion and disgusting in the community."

"What did Train do?"

"He consulted with the three of us again. We all knew about Simpson's problem; he had been a drinker for years and years. The question was, do you take formal action? Train said he had talked to him before about getting help. Simpson had promised, gone on the wagon for a time, but that didn't last long. This time Train wanted to give him a formal warning and, if he didn't straighten up, undertake some kind of formal action."

We all knew Lou Simpson. I had had him for Shakespeare. He was simply the best teacher I had ever had. He was a lush. Somebody had to haul him home from Clancy's or Jolly's at least once a month. Once when he was drunk, Simpson had intimated to me that he had known Bill a long time ago. I pressed him, but he refused to say anything more, and I let it go; it had been idle curiosity on my part. Where could he have known Train? Would anything in the past have triggered a murder? I realized I didn't know much about Bill's past. The usual administrative climb, a dean somewhere and then a vice chancellor somewhere in the South, or was it West? Maybe I should harass Hannah with questions like the sheriff.

"That it?" I said.

"All I can think of. If I can help you or the police in any way, don't hesitate to call on me."

"I won't," I said, and went, rather dampened, on my way to find Professor Polly Rector's office. Life in the university was beginning to sound like life in the rest of Silvertown. Hadn't we a right to expect more of university people than others, like the Jaycees?

51

# IX

Professor Polly Rector is six feet tall. Her face is round, and her bottom is even rounder; her arms and legs are round but pinched off at the wrists and elbows and ankles and knees, rather like German summer sausage. Her voice, if not rotund, is orotund, and she uses it to roll over those who dare speak on the opposing side of any question she espouses. And espouse she does—any and every lost or unpopular cause, whether meritorious or merely mischievous. To upbraid a male colleague for his stupidity going back to his birth appears to provide her the kind of pleasure many women receive in their marital (or extracurricular) beds.

But she can, unbelieveable as it sounds, be charming. She can sidle up to you (verbally), insinuate she is on your side against the army of idiots that surrounds us, and so include you in her small ken of clever and virtuous disciples. By the time you come to your senses, it is too late; you have been taken in.

When the expansions and contractions of her activities come to rest, however, her coterie consists of the chairman of the English Department, one or two other members of the English Department, a clarinet teacher from Music, and two gay blades from Art.

She lectures beautifully, but you must agree with her or flunk. Her undergraduate degree from Bryn Mawr and her Ph.D. from Harvard in American Literature are, surely, the most distinguished at Silvertown. She wrote her dissertation on Melville and has published one article. She may have felt some kinship with the Confidence Man. Or Captain Vere. Or the great white whale.

She had also published, with a small press in Oshkosh, a thin volume of poems. I don't read poetry myself, but those who do say the poems are very romantic and very bad.

I knew her from rumor (these were legion) and from personal experience. She and several misguided female students sued Dicky James and the Police Department for police brutality. The police had arrested a group of Rector's protesters who had disrupted a lecture and then physically attacked a speaker they considered both a male chauvinist pig and a warmonger. The students had kicked and bitten the security people and then the Silvertown Police when they were called. The Silvertown men in blue handled the women students as though they were men, by handcuffing them and hauling them forcibly to the city jail. Most of the students cooled off and were released on their recognizance, but several refused to be released and charged the police with molesting and "brutalizing" them.

At the time, I was city attorney (the Silvertown lawyers take turns in the job; it's a bit of a nuisance). Despite verbal harassment from Rector, I won the suit for the city, hands down, so to speak. We had enough witnesses and photographs taken by the local and student press to prove our case that nothing untoward had occurred except on the part of the small group of students toward the university's guest speaker. All that was a long time ago, in the time of general student unrest and our undeclared war in Vietnam.

53

While we had not quite made up, Polly Rector and I had a sort of undeclared truce. That still didn't mean I had to like her. Nor she me.

When I knocked at her open door, we greeted each other by first name. "Come in, Sean," she said.

"How are you, Polly," I inquired.

"How do you expect me to be?" she said. Her tone was more subdued than I had ever heard it—still acerb yet a bit sad.

When I gave her my story, she nodded. "I know," she said. "I've heard. How can I help you? You know I didn't agree with Bill Train about very much."

"But you knew him well, and you talked to him fairly frequently, I understand."

"He was a good man in many ways," she said. "He tried to do the right thing, but he got bad advice from Hartpence and Yeats and the deans. He didn't know what was going on in the departments. I tried to tell him." She turned toward the window, her eyes glistening.

I had never seen her this way. I was touched. Or was she taking me in? "Why would anyone want to bash his head in?" I said.

She shuddered; her whole round body seemed to fall in on itself. After a bit she said, "Whatever grievance one has, violence is not the way to redress it. People are strange, though. They can be seized by passions beyond their control. I've thought about it, but I can't tell you who might have done it. However, I have a suspicion." She hunched her large body up on the squeaking chair. "Train was involved in something more than Silvertown. I've thought that for a long time. He was involved in some kind of government stuff a long time ago, and it's my opinion he still was when he died. It would not surprise me if that was what led to his death."

"What sort of government stuff?"

"That's for you to find out, isn't it?"

"You're the one with the suspicions. What do you base them on?"

"I have friends who have hinted things. And there are other things."

"What have your friends hinted? What other things?"

"They have known him before, in previous incarnations, so to speak."

"Where? As what?"

"They didn't say, as I said. They hinted."

"What are the other things, then?"

She slumped down in the protesting chair, turned to the window. "One time when I was in his office—I had just popped in without an appointment—I saw some papers on the corner of his desk that had the word *Secret* marked on them in heavy black ink. He saw that I had seen them, and he covered them up with other papers as we talked."

"Did you ask him about them?"

"Yes, I did."

Knowing her, I knew she would. "What did he say?"

"He said they were secret."

"And you pressed him?"

"I asked him what a chancellor was doing with papers marked *Secret*."

"And?"

"He said they were secret."

"Unless the papers were purloined," I said, "he must have had some kind of clearance."

"You're not so dumb, after all."

"Did you see anything else on the papers beside *Secret*, like a logo, for example?"

"I didn't see anything else, but it has to be CIA, doesn't it?"

"Not necessarily. All kinds of government agencies mark documents secret."

"Well, I think this was CIA or some kind of secret agency stuff."

"Why would the chancellor at Silvertown have secret papers from a secret agency?"

"Good question. Find the answer to that, and maybe you'll find the answer to his murder."

"I'm not so sure." I said.

She pulled herself up in her customary orbicular hauteur and glared straight at me. "Why do you say that?"

"In the first place, the CIA and the other intelligence agencies do not, as a rule, assassinate people associated with them. And, secondly, it is a fairly accepted commonplace that agents of both friendly and enemy countries do not knock each other off. It would get to be a blood bath. They prefer just to know who they are—and they often do—and find out what they are up to."

"How do you know that?" she said.

"I read a lot of spy novels," I said.

She was not amused. "We're talking about the real world, Sean. You can't just throw out what I've told you. That has to be the background for what happened to Bill. What else is there?"

"A disgruntled faculty member or student. I think it's local." Actually, I didn't know what I thought at that point, but I wanted to push her.

"Bullshit," she said sonorously. I was sure her voice carried down the hall to the rest of the English Department. Probably they were used to hearing that fine old English expression.

"All right," I said. "Let's say you're right. How do I get ahold of some evidence?"

She leaned down in her chair again. It was a strong oak chair, with padding in the seat and back. Noisy but sturdy. "If I could get you some, would you keep my part in this confidential?"

"If he or she is not a party to a crime," I said, "I can keep the source of my information confidential."

"What the hell does that mean? Do you think I have committed or would commit a crime?"

"For a good cause, probably."

"I'm trying to be helpful, Sean. Don't give me any crap."

"I accept your help. I want to get to the bottom of this."

"I'll see what I can do," she said.

"By the way, were you on campus that Saturday?"

She set her jaw hard, causing her jowls to flap. "Yes, I was. Why do you ask?"

"For one thing, I wondered whether you saw anyone enter or leave the Administration Building."

"I was in my office," she announced acidly, "and my office is on the west side of this building, facing our glorious field house. For what other thing do you ask?"

"Were you in the Administration Building that day?"

Her eyes clouded over. "You can leave now," she said, almost absently.

# X

It occurred to me that Rector's source for hints about the chancellor's past might be Lou Simpson. He had, after all, dropped hints to some of us that he knew something or another. And, since I was in his corridor, I searched for his office (when I had taken him for Shakespeare long ago, his office had been in old Main where most of the faculty offices were then). His door was partly open, but no answer came when I knocked. I peeked in. No Professor Simpson. The place was a mess, books and papers everywhere, pictures of Shakespeare hanging at angles on the walls. The text on top of the pile was open to *Macbeth*. One story about him (there were many) was that he had reported his typewriter stolen. The security people had found it on his desk, under an Everest of paper.

I went to the department office, and there the secretary said he had already left. "Home?" I asked.

"Clancy's or Jolly's," she said, with a small smile.

I decided to try Clancy's before I climbed upstairs to Fogarty, Svenson and Bosch.

He was sitting at the bar with a shot glass of what I knew was straight volka in front of him. From the look of him as I sat down, it was not his first.

"How ya doin', Professor?" I asked.

"Why, Counselor Fogarty," he said. "I thought you lived on the second floor."

"If you wanna be the top banana," I said, "you gotta start on the first floor." I signaled to Clancy's son Jimmy who was playing barkeep.

"You know," Lou observed, squinting at me with his head drawn back, "you aren't any wittier now than when you took Shakespeare from me at nineteen."

Jimmy brought me Dewar's on the rocks. "I must have been pretty witty then, too."

Lou laughed. The thousand tiny wrinkles in his old face moved like ripples on a pond after a rock is thrown in.

"There's something I've been meaning to ask you ever since I took your course."

"What's that?"

"You gave me an A minus for the second semester."

"Mm."

"What was the minus for?"

"To keep you in your place, probably. My God, I can't remember that far back. But you would have deserved exactly what I gave you."

"I've got another question for you about something even farther back." I sipped my Dewar's.

"What's that?"

"You knew Bill Train a long time ago?"

"A fellow of infinite jest, of most excellent fancy," he said. He downed his vodka and pursed his lips. He took out a wrinkled handkerchief and blew his nose. As my eyes grew more accustomed to the dark, I could see that the wrinkles on his forehead had beads of sweat on them. "I don't think I should answer that question," he said.

"It's possible that Train's past may have something to do with his murder."

Lou waved at Jimmy. "It's possible, but I'm not the one to say."

"I'm looking into it for Hannah . . ."

"I know," he interrupted.

"Who told you?"

"It's a small town."

"If there is a connection, I need to know. And as far as I can tell, you're the only one in town who can enlighten me."

"What about Hannah?"

"She's having dinner with us tonight, I think, and I'll ask. But I want to know what you know."

"I'm sure she knows more about Train's past than I do." Jimmy poured another vodka into his shot glass. "And besides I'm not objective. I'm on his blacklist."

"The chancellor had a blacklist?"

"That's the rumor."

"Of what?"

"Of people he wanted to get rid of, one way or another."

"You believe that?"

"He was trying to get rid of me."

"You mean he warned you about your drinking problem."

"That's the way to get rid of me, isn't it?"

"Who else was on the list?"

"Good question."

A voice called out a greeting to me from the back of the room. It was Bobby Keyes, Silvertown's biggest independent insurance agent and wittiest wag. He was sitting under the moose head with a crew of local hunters and fishermen. I waved back. Clancy's Tavern sports one moose head, fifteen pairs of antlers, three big muskies, and a bear skin on its walls, a tribute to the prowess of our men with rods and guns. When I turned back to Lou, his new vodka was gone.

"Lou," I said, "I need this as a favor. I'll keep it confidential. I don't talk about what I know is nobody else's business, and I wouldn't ask if it weren't important. This is a matter of murder."

"A foul and most unnatural murder," he said.

He signaled to Jimmy. I sipped my Dewar's and waited. He was sweating. If I waited long enough, he might get drunk enough to tell me, but I had to get back to my office and then home to get ready for dinner.

"I've got a friend in Justice in Washington," I said. "I suppose he might be able to dig up something for me about you and Train."

Lou took me by the arm. "What do you mean about me? You're not interested in me."

"If you and Train knew each other in some capacity in the past, it might be pertinent to what happened to him, might it not? I have to look at every angle."

He took out his handkerchief and blew his nose again. Jimmy filled his glass again and he quaffed it fast. "You have no right to look into my past. I had nothing to do with Train's murder."

"I don't think you do, but I have to be sure, don't I? And, in any case, you have information that might reveal some connections that might in fact have to do with his murder."

"That's all speculation," Lou said. His speech was beginning to slur just a little. When he pursed his lips and failed to unpurse them, it was the sure sign he had reached his top state of intoxication, which was usually followed by falling on the floor. At this point, however, it was merely sweat and slurred words.

"It's speculation until I am sure it pertains or does not, and I can't tell that until I have the facts I need. Lou," I took his arm now, "I need your help. If you tell me what I need to know, I won't have to call my friend at Justice."

"You're a bastard, Sean, you know that?" His esses had dropped to lisps.

61

"Only when I have to be."

"All right. All right," he said. He signaled to Jimmy.

I sipped my Dewar's and waited.

"I knew Bill a long time ago. Germany. Occupation. Army Intelligence. I was a sergeant; he was a lieutenant. Even though he was younger than I, he was my boss even then. He already had a master's degree. He spoke German very well, and he had studied the German philosophers. He understood the Germans, and he could get information from them because they thought he was sympathetic. He did evaluations of German political activity. He kept his eye on the old Nazis and the leftists that were coming out from under the rocks. He went into East Germany and ran some agents there. Then they shipped me back." Jimmy poured a new vodka.

"Your enlistment ran out?"

His eyes were beginning to glaze. He looked down at his glass. "Yeah, sure." He swallowed the vodka.

"And Train?"

"He was still there when I went home."

"What happened to him after that?"

"I don't know. The next time I saw him was when he came to Silvertown as chancellor."

"I understand he was wounded."

"Yeah, thass right. East Germany. He came back, and they put him in the hospital. He was there when I left."

"He was wounded in East Germany?"

"Thass right."

"After the war."

"Yeah." He pursed his lips. The sweat was pouring down his face. He took out his handkerchief and wiped his face and blew his nose, more or less at the same time.

"Of course," he said, "you know about Laurence and Bella Leiberman."

"They teach languages?"

"Thass right. They're refugees from the People's Republic of Germany. Bill brought them here. He teaches German. She teaches Russian."

"Did Bill know them before?"

Lou shrugged and pursed his lips again. "Interestink qvestion, ja?"

"Is that all you know?"

"Thass right." He signaled Jimmy. Jimmy was shaking his head at me.

I patted him on the arm. "Time to go home," I said.

"You go," he said. "I schtay. Give me the cup: lesh go; by heaven, I'll have't."

I got up and walked to the cash register. I dropped a twenty on the counter. "I'll pay, but he's about had it," I said.

"I think so, too," Jimmy said. He handed me a ten back.

"I'm dead, Horatio," Lou said.

Bobby Keyes yelled at me as I passed. "Did you hear about the North Dakota woman whose daughter called and said she was pregnant?"

"No," I said dutifully. "What did the North Dakota woman say to her daughter who was pregnant?"

"She said, 'My God, are you sure it's yours?' " He leaned back, and everybody laughed with beery gusto.

# XI

Well, I was pregnant with quintuplets, and I didn't know who the father of any one of them was, I thought as I scaled the heights from Clancy's to my office. Among the messages was one from Susie, saying that yes, Hannah was coming to dinner and I should come home in time to get ready. And one from Betty Olson saying Acting Chancellor Hartpence had given her permission to show me the nasty alumnus letter. That would have to wait until tomorrow. I made a few calls, told Julie to keep things quiet for me for the next several days, and went home. It's Bill that's dead, Horatio, I said to myself. And no ghost to tell me who has done it.

I like to go home. Susie and I rehash our days' activity over a cocktail, with pertinent interpolations. And she's a good cook when she chooses to be. She was in the midst of taking her incomparable cheesecake out of its pan when I arrived. I offered to test it to make sure it was all right, but she refused my offer.

"Go take your shower and put on some clean clothes," she said. "I told Hannah it would be casual, so you can wear a sports jacket." She sniffed, as I kissed her. "You've had a drink already."

"In the line of duty," I said.

Our house is an old Victorian, which we remodeled.

64

We added a master bedroom suite when Cathy started high school and gave her the big old upstairs bedroom. The shower was built to my specifications (Susie designed the kitchen), plenty of room and the shower head high enough so that I don't have to kneel to get under it to wash my hair. Most showers are made for women and midgets.

The shower felt good, and I let it run for a while, rinsing away some of the crud that stuck to me after talking with Penney and Rector and poor old Simpson and hearing about Wallace and Richards. I was beginning to regret I had agreed to get into the investigation. The sheriff was right; it was none of my damned business. I was ready for a real drink by the time I marched back into the kitchen.

"I'm ready for a real drink," I said.

"Wait for Hannah," Susie said. "She'll be here shortly. She's always on time." She shook water from the salad greens. "What did you find out today?"

"Too much," I said. "I've got more suspects than I could check out in ten years." I recounted with lawyerly brevity what I had learned from and about the day's assortment of misfits.

"You may have a likely candidate in *that* bunch," Susie said.

"Or I may not," I said.

The front doorbell rang.

Hannah Train is tall, dark-haired, elegant. She has a slightly foreign accent, the result, I had figured, of growing up in the East and going to Smith, but Susie said Hannah had been born in Germany. She makes being fifty look like being forty. She always wore long-sleeved dresses, Susie had remarked once, admiringly. Most of the women of Silvertown liked her, I gather, even when they were envious of her position. She filled her position with ease and put others at ease. The Trains were not members of the old aristocracy in Silvertown; they were not natives.

The Nate Colbys were the old upper crust. The chancellor and his wife were, by virtue of their position and the importance of the university to the economy, in the upper levels of the bourgeoisie. After all, the chancellor was a salaried state employee; he did not live on banking or lumber or investment income. The Trains dined with regional politicians and saw the governor more often than did the Colbys. (The governor, indeed, had sent an aide to represent him at the funeral. The regional legislators had attended, of course; in our sparsely populated area, they go to any event where there's a crowd.) The Trains had less access to those with money in the state than the Colbys, more access to those in political power. We in the bourgeoisie dealt professionally with the Colbys (and with extreme care, holding tight to our shirts); we preferred the company of the Trains.

It should be said that the Trains seemed completely unconcerned with our small-town sociology. They cared about the university and cultivated the sources of its welfare: the university system senior officers, the Regents, legislators, the governor, potential donors among the alumni. They had their friends across the country, we gathered from references now and then, but in Silvertown they were self-contained, friendly toward all who wished to be friendly and even some who did not, friends with their friends. They ignored the innuendoes of local caste.

We had not seen Hannah socially since the funeral, and we embraced warmly. I got our drinks, a Martini straight up for Hannah. She seemed under less strain than at the funeral, but she was still hollow of cheek, and her eyes were misty after we embraced.

She asked after Cathy; we asked after the Train sons, one in graduate school at Berkeley, one in business in San Diego. It was obvious she was still trying to sort her life out. She planned to stay in Silvertown for a while and put the house on the market. They had built a contemporary on Lake Arrowhead at the edge of town. The older son had insisted she come out to San Diego. She thought she might do that next winter, but she didn't want to put her sons in the position of feeling they had to attend to her.

"Why not just stay here in Silvertown?" Susie said. "You have many friends here."

"I don't think I can," Hannah said. "I need to get away from where . . . it happened."

There was nothing to say to that; it was understandable. Since we had come to "what had happened," I unfolded my activities of the last two days, except for the papers and for Bill's intelligence role in the war. She gathered that the police had not made much progress; she did not object that I had extended my mandate from her to represent her to making inquiries.

I held off mentioning the papers and what I had learned from Lou Simpson until we had finished dinner. We returned to the living room with deserved praise for Susie's cheesecake and sipped our coffee. Since Hannah seemed almost relaxed, I hesitated to bring the circumstance of the murder up again, but she was the person who might be able to clear up some of the mystery.

When I told her about Fountain's story of the messy papers, she seemed genuinely puzzled. She said she hadn't seen any papers, but of course she had been too shaken to see anything except Bill. What I had learned from Simpson was not new to her.

"I knew about Bill's mission during the Occupation, though he didn't tell me about running agents in East Germany, and I'm not sure that's true. And I knew he had been wounded, but I thought that happened in West Germany. That was all so long ago, what could it have to do with his murder?"

"It might have nothing at all to do with it," I said. "Was

Bill working on any project that you were aware of, a scholarly project, or something for the government?"

"Not that I'm aware of. He worked on articles from time to time."

"Do you think that the papers Fountain saw were some kind of government project?" She seemed puzzled again, and her coffee cup was perfectly steady in her hand.

I told her then about Polly Rector seeing a document marked *Secret* on his desk.

"I can't believe that," she said. "And I would not entirely trust Polly. It just doesn't make sense for Bill to have a secret document of some sort, at least marked that way. I'm sure there were personnel matters that were secret, and sometimes political things, preliminary budgets, strategy papers for dealing with the legislature that the university system people and the chancellors were considering, but beyond that I can't imagine anything secret that Bill would have to do with." She put her cup down and shook her head when Susie asked if she would like a refill.

"Any more of your good coffee, and I won't be able to sleep. I should be going soon, anyway."

She started to say something more when we heard a crash and breaking glass from the direction of the kitchen. We were all startled, and I was on my feet without realizing I had stood up.

"Stay here," I said. I walked quickly into the kitchen. The women had not followed my order; they were at my shoulder when we saw the tube on the kitchen floor in the midst of shattered glass. It had obviously been thrown through the window, through which cold air blew, making physical what we were feeling psychologically.

"Go back into the living room," I said. "It may be a pipe bomb."

"You come back to the living room," Susie said. "Don't be a hero. Let's call the police."

68

"The Silvertown police don't have a bomb squad." I said. "Go into the living room."

The tube was covered with a thin white paper like Christmas wrapping. Hardly a customary service with pipe bombs. Maybe to disguise its transport?

Susie was hanging onto my arm and pulling. I shook loose and pushed them into the living room. Against Susie's protests, I went back into the kitchen and looked more closely at the tube. There was no sound of ticking, but that was not necessarily a sign there was no timing device. It might, of course, be detonated by remote control. I hurried to the garage, found a flat-bladed shovel, returned to the kitchen, and slid it under the tube gingerly. I backed gently toward the kitchen door, opening it with one hand behind me, stepped down and out, glided across the ghostly lawn like an extra in the *Nutcracker Suite,* and lowered the tube into the fish pond as gently as a newborn baby into its first crib. I jogged to the house, shivering from the cold and a small, explicable case of the jitters. It couldn't be real, I said to myself.

"What in heaven's name are you doing?" Susie demanded.

"I read somewhere that water dampens the tendency for certain kinds of explosives to explode."

"You're crazy," she said.

"At last you know," I said. I pushed her into the kitchen with Hannah and closed the door. I guess I wanted to see if anything would happen.

I found myself sitting on the ground before I heard the explosion. I had been showered with water. The explosion was curiously dull in sound, I thought somewhere in my brain. Susie and Hannah were on their knees beside me, inquiring as to my health.

"I'm all right, I think," I said. "It's just that my spirits are dampened."

69

"You could have been killed," Susie said.

That was truer than I had heretofore been prepared to acknowledge. Had I just been lucky with the timing? The lateral forces of the explosion, with metal fragments flung outward, had been contained by the sides of the fish pond. Or had the timing been by remote control? I had saved our kitchen and endangered my skin.

Though I seemed whole, Susie and Hannah helped me to my feet. It was then we noticed the paper tacked to the back door. Hannah pulled the tack and brought the paper to the kitchen counter where we gathered to read its neatly hand-printed block letters: THIS IS A WARNING. MIND YOUR OWN DAMNED BUSINESS.

Did that mean they (whoever they were, was) could have killed me but were (this time) merely warning me? If they intended to, it would be easy. Did the threat include Susie?

Had they given the chancellor a warning before they (he, she) bashed his skull in for ignoring it? What might he have discovered? What was I finding that might kill me?

# XII

Susie and Hannah remained upset. I warmed myself with dry duds and double Dewar's on the rocks. "It's a good sign I'm making progress in some direction or another. Trouble is I'm not sure which direction."

"How can you say that?" Susie said. "We've just had our lives threatened."

"If someone didn't think I was getting close to him, or her, he or she wouldn't try to warn me off."

"That's progress?" Susie said.

"Sort of," I said. "And now we've also got some pieces of material evidence."

"The note?" Hannah said.

"Right. I don't suppose the Silvertown Police can do much in the way of identifying paper and hand-printing, but Sheriff Anderson said the State Criminal Investigation Bureau is on the case. They ought to be able to do some lab work on the bomb fragments and the note."

"Providing they are cooperative," Susie said. "The sheriff didn't seem very enthusiastic about cooperating with you last night at Jolly's."

"Ah, well, he can't really ignore this, no matter how much he agrees with the sentiment the note expresses."

"Maybe he sent it," Susie said. I knew she was recovering.

We were standing in the kitchen looking at the note. I had tacked a piece of cardboard over the broken window. Susie and Hannah were drinking brandy.

"It's very nicely printed," Hannah observed.

"Even artistic," I said.

"Somebody who knows a good deal about printing by hand," Susie said.

"It ought to be identifiable," I said.

"Unless it's disguised," Hannah said.

"The paper looks like ordinary bond typing paper," Susie said.

"We'll look for a watermark," I said. "I'm sure there are fingerprints, especially after it's been handled by all of us."

"You were very courageous, Sean," Hannah said.

"You were extremely foolhardy," Susie said.

"I prefer the first opinion," I said.

"What are you going to do do?" Hannah said.

"Pursue my list of suspects, endless as it seems to be. Add any more that seem likely. Try to follow up on the mystery of the messy papers. So far I've been looking for motive and asked very little about opportunity. I need to ask about opportunity. If I keep pushing, we may get another break like the note."

"Break?" Susie said.

Hannah turned thoughtful. "Sean," she said, "maybe the message is good advice. I would hate myself forever if you two got hurt in any way trying to help me. Whatever one may think of Bert Anderson, he is a policeman, and so is Dicky James, and so are the people in the Criminal Investigation Bureau. Wouldn't it be wiser to let them carry this on? You've apparently stirred something up. Let them follow up."

"It's not only for you, Hannah; it's for me. I don't want to let some crazy person get away with what he did to a good friend of mine, to the chancellor of my university. Nor do I intend to be intimidated. Maybe the sheriff and the chief and the Criminal Investigation people can solve it, but I don't intend to stand by while they fail. I'll give them what I find. They may not return the favor, but that's O.K. I'm sticking with this thing now until we find the murderer or until we have exhausted ourselves trying."

Hannah finished her brandy and hugged me. We saw her to the door and said our good-byes. Her eyes were a little misty again. "Thank you," she said, "for being such good friends."

# XIII

Brave words after Dewar's on the rocks in the evening, sober doubts about how to go about living up to them in the morning. After a restless night, Susie served up more qualms with scrambled eggs. The weather turned back to winter, the way it does in northern Wisconsin in the spring. I drove to work in my four-wheel drive, just in case.

I sat in my office and brooded for a while. I had Julie make a Xerox of the bomb note. On a sheet of legal-size paper I put down the names I had, in no particular order:

    Pickel & wife
    Pickel jock-sniffers
    Fountain
    Penney
    Richards
    Wallace
    Simpson
    Hartpence
    Rector
    Former Dean Nelson
    Hank Green
    Dismissed student

Removed secretary and spouse
Women's Studies
CIA
KGB
East German KGB

Then I added:

Hannah Train

I felt a little foolish adding Hannah's name, but it seemed the sheriff had her on his list. I buzzed Julie to get Rusty Yeats and Dicky James for me and to try to set up appointments for me with Professor Richards of the Sociology Department and Professor Wallace of Math. And to try Women's Studies again. I needed to find out the name of that secretary whose husband was so angry when Bill had shifted her out of his office. Rusty would know her name, too. I needed to check out opportunity for each and every one on my list. Fountain had the opportunity; he was on duty on the campus that day and in possession of master keys to let him in anywhere. Penney said he had an alibi, a slew of relatives. Would the relatives lie for him? That should be checked.

Simpson could not have thrown the pipe bomb through my window; he was soused when I left him, wasn't he? Hannah could not have thrown it; she was sitting in the living room with Susie and me. (Did the murderer, or murderess, have an accomplice?)

Rusty came on the line. "Did you find out the name of that student who was dismissed and threatened Bill?"

"Just got it about a minute ago," Rusty said. "It's Nick Lee. The home address we have for him in our files is Milwaukee. I've got it here somewhere. Ah, yes." He read off the address and a phone number. "Of course, we don't know whether he's living at home."

"O.K., thanks," I said. "Do you remember the name of the secretary that Bill removed and put somewhere else the first year he was here? As I remember it, her husband was sore as hell."

"That was Maria Thompson. Her husband is David. He worked for the university on our maintenance crew. He just retired on disability this year. She's still working in the Math Department."

"What is David's disability?"

"Leukemia."

"Unh," I said. "What's the prognosis?"

"Six months, maybe. Of course, leukemia is funny, you can have remissions, and he had one already, last year. But I hear it's pretty bad right now."

"They don't sound like they could manage a murder."

"I think not."

"Did the chancellor have a blacklist?"

"A blacklist? What for?"

"People he wanted to get rid of."

"There were a few people he thought ought to go, but I don't know of any blacklist."

"Had any further ideas?"

"No. I guess not."

We hung up. I asked Julie to try the phone number of Nick Lee in Milwaukee.

Julie rang and said she had Milwaukee. I pressed the flashing button. "Hello?"

"Hello," a female voice.

"Is Nick Lee there?"

"No, he ain't."

"Can you tell me where I can reach him?"

"I don't know. He's up in northern Wisconsin, in Silvertown. I don't have no telephone number for him there. He's staying with friends."

Whoof! That was interesting. "Do you know the names of his friends?"

"No. They students there."

"Thank you very much."

I barely had time to catch my breath when Chief Dicky James came on. I asked if I could buy him some lunch about noon.

"Are you trying to bribe me?" he said.

"Of course," I said.

"That case you can buy me a good lunch at Harry's Hideaway."

"Good. I'll see you at noon," I said.

Julie reported that Professor Wallace was on sabbatical and did not go to his office this semester, but she had reached him at home, and he said he would see me there at two. He had asked what it was about, but Julie had said she didn't know and I was on another line. He said he would see me anyway.

I dialed Rusty again and told him about Nick Lee being in town. He whistled. I asked him how I could find out where he was staying.

"We don't have many black students, and they are mostly female," he said. "Of course he might be staying with a female. Men students have been known to stay with women students, even in the dorms. I'll see if I can find out where he might be. Dean Ammons would probably have an idea. I'm sure he remembers Nick Lee. I'll call you back."

I had to get my mind clear, so I worked on some contracts for timber purchases I had to have ready for next week, until Horace Blackbothom came by with a petition. He comes by with a petition at least once a month. Horace is ninety, sharp as a tack, and takes a persistent interest in the doings of the city manager and the city council. He writes letters to the editor of the *Silvertown Bee* and gets up petitions at every hint of wrongdoing. If our politicians can't get away with any shenanigans, we owe it to Horace. His latest petition asked for a recall of the city manager. I signed it. I sign all his petitions. I also draw up a new will for him at least every other month. Horace has a substantial investment in real estate, and everybody wants it: the Lutheran church, the Methodist church, the University Development Office, the Silvertown Hospital Association, various younger women he takes out to dinner at Jolly's, and the Hospice for Unwed Mothers. He changes his mind as often as the wind blows from the northwest. Horace keeps me up on the latest political news and his amatory outings. I listened until noon.

Harry's Hideaway is actually in the basement of Clancy's; the building is on a slope so that the entrance is on street level on First Street. I have to go around the block to get there, and I do frequently when I don't go home for lunch. Harry's has the best cook in town: Harry. He does steaks and prime rib to perfection. A small prime rib sandwich at noon is the favorite of a lot of businessmen. A big one at noon would put you to sleep for the afternoon. Dicky was already there having his usual light beer.

"Some people have been calling me asking whether you've joined the police force," Dicky said.

"I trust you told them I'm your star detective."

"I said you're the best man in plainclothes in town."

"Well, the bad guys have identified me," I said. I related the events of the previous evening.

Dicky heard me with a face turned serious and demanded to know why I hadn't notified him at once.

"It was too dark to collect any evidence," I said. "And I didn't want a lot of commotion. Your people can go over this afternoon quietly and collect bomb fragments and such. And here is the note with the friendly advice." I handed him the paper from the kitchen door.

Dicky excused himself and went to the phone box by the front entrance. He returned and examined the note, holding it up to the light.

"We might be able to identify the hand-printing," he said. "We'll have to send whatever is left from the bomb to the State Police lab. Damn it, Sean, I don't like this at all."

A student came to take our orders. Harry supports the university by hiring and firing student waitresses. We ordered prime rib sandwiches. I recounted then my somewhat milder adventures in interviewing, omitting, as I had promised, Rector's offer to find me some evidence of CIA involvement.

Dicky was thoughtful. "Maybe you should heed the note's advice, Sean."

"Because I'm getting close to something?"

"Because somebody thinks you're meddling."

"Should I take the threat seriously?"

"Take all threats seriously until proven innocent. I'll have a squad car keep an eye on your house for a while. We can't keep one parked there; we don't have enough. One will drive by frequently and sit there at different times on an irregular basis. We have more than enough lawyers in town, but I wouldn't want anything to happen to Susie."

"I appreciate the protection."

"Least we can do."

"Where do you think I've gotten close?"

He thought about it and sipped the rest of his Miller Lite. "Maybe just poking around, maybe one of the people you talked to, maybe one of the people you asked about. Hard to say, really."

"You're a real help."

"I'm careful about jumping to conclusions."

"You must have some ideas."

"Yeah."

"Well?"

"I don't speculate about suspects until I have some evidence."

"Do you have some evidence?"

"Counselor, I'm not on the stand."

"You were once when I questioned you."

Dicky laughed. "Yeah, I remember that. You did a good job questioning everybody. I'll tell you one thing, and you keep it under your hat. It may or may not have anything to do with the chancellor's murder. Fountain did see some papers there. They were removed. I can't tell you anything more than that, and I didn't tell you that. You already knew it. Don't ask me anything more about it."

"Who can I ask about it?"

"You'll have to figure that out for yourself."

The coed came with our prime rib sandwiches.

I didn't get anything more out of Dicky. I had given him something, I wasn't sure what. He had given me a little something, I wasn't sure what. He promised to send the bomb fragments to Madison, to see what the crime lab could do with them. He didn't expect much. He thought maybe I could do something with the fancy printing. He looked worried. And puzzled. By something that didn't fit with what he did know about? He said to take care, looking at me hard. I left twenty percent for the coed.

As I came around the block, I saw Lou Simpson in the window of Jim Merrill's bookstore. He waved at me to come in. He was pale but sober; it was a school day and early in the afternoon.

"You're on the wrong track, Counselor," he said. "The word around campus is that it has to be Hartpence." The

light from a moment of afternoon sun through the bookstore window printed a *Sale* sign on his face.

"Why Hartpence?"

"The consensus is that he has the most to gain and that
he got tired of waiting for Train to leave or retire. And,
of course, there is that rumor about his first wife."

"What rumor about his first wife?"

"That his first wife died under mysterious circumstances."

"What mysterious circumstances?"

"The cause of her death is unknown."

"Where did that rumor come from?"

"Apparently from Hartpence himself."

"What do you think?"

"Could be."

"What else does the grapevine say?"

"That you were hired by Hannah Train to track down
the killer and that Dicky James has deputized you."

"Want to see my star?"

"No thanks. I've already seen it."

"Sorry about that, Lou. I needed the information."

"Yeah, sure."

My eye caught a small stack of thin books in magenta
covers with Polly Rector's name on the spine. I thanked
Lou for his report from the grapevine and went over to
examine *The Cry of the Dove.* I thumbed gingerly through
several pages.

"They're awful," Lou said over my shoulder.

They were. Shelley had been bad enough when I had to
read him for my English major, but this stuff made Harry's
prime rib sandwich turn over in my stomach like Mc-
Donald's gristle. Thees and thous, declarations of passion-
ate love sprinkled with images of several species of flowers
and trees, tropes from tropical seas and distant stars. Polly
with a lover? It was simply daydreaming in bad taste,

wasn't it? What a curiously vulnerable side to such a tough-talking, gross woman! I put the book down carefully. The binding was as fragile as the poems.

"Not buying?" Lou said.

"Not my kind of stuff," I said.

"What is your kind of stuff? The Grand Inquisitor scene from *The Brothers Karamazov*?"

"No," I said. "*Much Ado About Nothing,* by Francis Bacon."

# XIV

Meanwhile, back at the office, there was a message from Rusty. Dean Ammons had done some digging and come up with the name and address of Nick Lee's girlfriend. She was living in an upstairs apartment on Hickory Street with another female student. No phone. Ammons said she was an honors student. Ironic pairing.

Steven Wallace lived just out of town on the state highway that eventually connects with the interstate into Madison. The south part of town along the highway has collected the excrescence of all the franchised junk foods known to man: McDonald's, Kentucky Fried Chicken, A&W Root Beer, Dairy Queen, Wendy's, Dunkin' Donuts, Taco Bell, Pizza Hut, Shakey's Pizza, ad nauseam. Add to that the K-Mart, all the used car lots and gas stations that prey on tourists in the summer and students the rest of the year, and you know where you are: in the middle of the American Dream.

A *For Sale* sign was planted in the front yard of the Wallace house, a white clapboard on an acre at the corner of an empty hayfield. Wallace met me in jeans and a sweatshirt. The house was cold. Wallace is short, dark, and handsome, in his mid-forties. Was it the change of life that led him to the desperation of trying to seduce his young students? Or the good old tradition of macho professors who are not good at anything else? He didn't exactly welcome me, but he did open the door wide enough for me to enter.

"The house is not in very neat condition," he said. "As you can see, I'm getting ready to move."

There were boxes stacked in the living room, almost blocking the furniture. He motioned me into the family room, where a wood fire was burning in the fireplace. The central heat was apparently turned off.

"My wife and family are visiting her mother," he added.

I wondered if the visit were permanent. "I'm sorry to bother you in the midst of all this," I said. "I've been retained by Mrs. Train to find out all I can about her husband's death."

He did not seem surprised. Perhaps the grapevine had reached him, too.

"I don't think I can help you," he said.

"I am aware of the reason you are leaving," I said. "And I will keep it confidential."

He gave me a hostile look.

"I can understand that you may not have had very good feelings about Chancellor Train."

"Oh, you can, can you? How would you feel if you had been framed?"

"If I were framed, I would not feel very good about it. Were you framed?"

"I sure as hell was."

"By whom?"

"By Train. And some students who didn't like the grades I gave them." His dark face had taken on the look of aggrieved petulance.

"I really don't know the details of the case, Professor Wallace. My concern is with your possible reaction to it."

"I didn't kill Train, if that's what you want to know."

"You might have felt you had a motive."

84

"No doubt about that, but I didn't. My life is in shambles as it is. Why would I want to make it worse?"

"Vengeance, perhaps. Anger sometimes leads a man to do things that may not be to his best advantage."

"Well, I am angry, all right, but I didn't do it."

"Where were you that Saturday between twelve and two?"

"Packing. And my wife was here with me."

"Anyone else see you at that time?"

"Nobody else offered to help us pack."

"Where's your wife?"

"I told you. With her mother in Peoria."

"Where are you moving to?"

"I have a job in another state."

"Where?"

"None of your business."

"Did you think of hiring a lawyer to defend you against the charges Train made?"

"Are you offering your services?"

"I don't solicit business. Did you think of contesting the charges?"

"With that kind of thing, you can't win. Committees always leak. And if I had appealed to the Regents, the leaks there would have gotten into the papers. Even if I could succeed in refuting the charges, my reputation would go down the drain."

"Why would Train have wanted to frame you?"

"He wanted to placate the women activists on the campus. They're the ones who put the students up to it. And he could save a tenured position to give to some other department."

"I hadn't noticed that Train was lacking in courage."

"Had you noticed that he was political?"

"Did you argue the matter with him?"

"No."

"Why not?"

"It was useless. He showed me the list of witnesses that were prepared to testify. It went way back to the other time."

"What other time?"

He appeared regretful that he had mentioned it. He shrugged. "Three years ago they tried it, too."

"What happened then?"

"Some female students said I'd made passes at them and promised them high grades if they submitted. It was a big lie then, too."

"What did the chancellor do at that time?"

"He gave me a warning. I argued with him that time, but he just said if the charges were false I wouldn't have to worry about the situation being repeated. If they were after me, why wouldn't it be repeated?"

"Who is *they?*"

"The women activists. A bunch of lesbians and communists."

"Lesbians and communists? I thought communists didn't tolerate sexual deviation?"

"Oh, shit. Look around you, man. Look at the campus. Look at Madison."

"I guess I don't see very well."

"You're an asshole."

"Am I a communist, too?"

"It wouldn't surprise me. All I know for sure is that you're an asshole."

"Why do you say that?"

"Because you're dumb. You can't see what's going on around you."

"What's going on around me?"

"If you're too dumb to see, I'm not going to tell you."

"Do you think the commies ought to be cleaned out?"

"Damn right."

"The Women's Studies group are communist?"

"Damn right."

"Train was a communist?"

"Oh, no, you don't. Look, I don't have to put up with you. Why don't you just leave?"

"You want me to leave?"

"Yeah, right now."

"Did Train deserve to die?"

"Just get out of my house."

"Or what?"

"Try to stay and see."

I decided not to.

# XV

On the way back to my office, I detoured to Hickory Street, the end of it owned by City Councilman "Jerky" Gershwin, Silvertown's most prominent slumlord. I ascended the rickety outside stairway to the second floor of a sagging Victorian. Barn-red paint was coming off in liberal peels. It was at least two minutes and several raps before the door opened a crack. A handsome black face peeked through the narrow opening.

"What do you want?" she said.

"I'm looking for Nick Lee," I said.

"He doesn't live here," she said.

"His mother said he was visiting here."

She looked surprised. "His mother?" She laughed. "His mother's dead."

"Then his sister. I called Milwaukee. A woman answered the phone and said he was visiting here."

"Well, he isn't here."

I caught a glimpse of someone moving behind her.

"I need to talk to him."

"He isn't here."

"Where can I find him?"

"I don't know."

"Shall I come back later?"

"What for?"

"I need to talk to Nick."

"He know you?"

"No. My name is Fogarty. I'm an attorney."

"What do you want to talk to him for?"

"About the death of the chancellor."

She stared at me in alarm. The door had drifted open a little more. The room was dark, but I thought I could see an inner door closing slowly.

"Well, he isn't here."

"All right," I said. "I'll come back later."

"He won't be here then either," she said, and closed the door.

I climbed down the rickety stairs, got in my four-wheel drive and drove around the corner and stopped out of sight of the house. I walked between the house on the corner and the next so that I came up behind the garage of the house I had just visited. There was a white Camaro sitting in the drive behind the house where the drive curved toward the garage. I leaned against the back of the garage and waited. In a few minutes I heard some heels clicking down the stairs. A car door slammed. I peeked around the corner of the garage. A young black man was revving the Camaro and craning his neck to see out his rearview mirror. He backed out of my sight. I heard the car hit the street and take off with a squeal of tires.

I drove back downtown to my office and called Dicky James. I told him about Nick Lee and gave him the license plate number of the white Camaro. He said he would ask his squad cars to keep a lookout for it and let me know where they saw it. It might be halfway to Milwaukee by now, of course.

Julie had another message from Betty Olson and a message from Polly Rector saying she had something for me if I would stop by her office.

I parked in a faculty slot. My four-wheel drive doesn't

carry the special alumni sticker. I'd have to take my chances. I could smell snow in the air as I fended my way through students changing classes toward Kinkaid Hall.

Rector was talking to a student. I waited in the corridor. Emil Dickinson, chairman of English, stalked down the corridor, bony and unkempt. He leaned his head to one side.

"Well," he said in his nasal New England tone. "To what do we owe the honor of your presence in the halls of learning?" He was trying to be jocular.

"I'm taking depositions from your staff as to your scholarly behavior," I said.

"Haw, haw," he said. He leaned on down the corridor toward the men's room.

The student left, firm admonitions still debouching from Rector's office. I poked my head in. She got up, waved me in, and closed the door. From under a stack of books she drew out a plain brown manila envelope.

"You promised confidentiality," she said.

"Within the law," I said.

She hesitated, then handed me the envelope. I thanked her. She opened the door for me.

The envelope tucked under my arm, I pushed my way through the rising cold to my vehicle. No ticket. The first flake whirled across my windshield as I drove to my office. "April in Silvertown," I crooned, to the tune of "April in Paris."

Once in my office and somewhat warmer, I opened the envelope and slid the contents onto my desk. The first sheet was Xeroxed, clearly a page of something longer. It was in German. I struggled for a sentence and gave up. The second page was a translation. Rector was being helpful as hell. I read it through twice and figured out it was a report of anti-state activities in the city of Leipzig perpetrated by capitalist lackeys, the family of a Nazi war criminal still being sought.

I checked in my trusty Hammond World Atlas and confirmed that Leipzig is in East Germany, as I suspected.

I asked Julie to call Sheriff Anderson. She reported back at once that the sheriff was in Madison and wouldn't be back until the following morning. I asked her to set up an appointment with him for me as early in the morning as he was likely to be in his office.

I'd had enough. I went home. Susie poured a Dewar's over rocks for me and chablis for herself. She had a casserole in the oven that would be ready in an hour. I recounted my day.

"So you've got three suspects," she said.

"What do you mean three? Which three?"

"Wallace. He sounds really crazy. Nick Lee. A foreign agent. Unless Bill was a spy for East Germany, and it's one of our agents."

"I've got more suspects than that," I said.

"Who?"

I read her my list. She laughed at some of the list but was aghast at my adding Hannah's name.

"That's absolutely ridiculous," she said.

"Most murders are committed by relatives, wives, brothers, uncles, close friends, or lovers."

"You're talking about people who quarrel and fight each other violently as a matter of rule, not someone like the Trains."

"We don't know for sure about their private life."

"We do, too. They were very happy together."

"Maybe he had a mistress in Madison."

"Don't be ridiculous. Bill wouldn't do that. Besides, Madison is small as Silvertown when it comes to everybody knowing everything anybody who is anybody does."

91

"Say that again."

"I can't."

She became pensive. "Do you think it could be a spy thing?"

"I don't know. Not for sure, anyway."

"But you have an idea?"

"I have some ideas. How was your day?"

"Cathy called."

"During the day, when I'm not here?"

"Yes."

"What's up?"

"She wants to come home."

"My God, why?"

"She's unhappy."

"With Connecticut College?"

"Not really the college."

"Well, what's it about?"

"She's in a kind of sophomore depression, I think. For one thing."

"And another thing?"

"She's got boyfriend trouble, I think."

"If some college jock is giving her trouble, I'll kill him."

"Sean, women have to go through all these kinds of things. It's part of growing up."

"Oh, sure. Spock for college kids. What did he do? Who is he?"

"He's a senior. I guess they got kind of close and then he dropped her, said he had to concentrate on his studies so he could get into medical school, and medical school would take a long time, was a grind, and all that."

"How close?"

"I don't know. Pretty close, I guess."

"Damn."

"Sean, she's twenty years old."

"Yeah? What were you doing at twenty?"

"You know very well. And we didn't tell anybody either."

"I didn't give you any line about having to concentrate on my studies."

"I don't remember you concentrating on your studies to begin with."

"Not when you were around. Damn it, Susie, I don't want Cathy to get hurt."

"You can't grow up for her, Sean. She's pretty solid, you know. She'll make it. I told her to think about it."

"What did she say?"

"She said she'd think about it."

We had the casserole and watched the news. Susie's sister called, and they talked for an hour. I tried to sort out what I had learned. We went to bed, waking up now and then, listening for breaking glass. Once I got up and saw a police cruiser sitting under the maple tree in front of the house. Good old Dicky James. I slept better after that.

# XVI

There was an inch of snow on the ground, and the wind was whirling it around in little spirals across the lawns and streets as I walked from my office to the Lost County courthouse. I had my winter down parka back on, and I was wishing I had a son who lived in San Diego who would invite us out for the winter. And the spring.

The sheriff's office is on the first floor of the courthouse. It's as big as a barn with twenty-foot ceilings. There are citations on the wall for this and that, and a pair of antlers above the sheriff's head. His head would look good between them.

"What can I do for you, Counselor?" Bert said in his customary affable tone. He was wearing his uniform today. Maybe his leisure suit was at the cleaners.

"You didn't have to go to such extremes to warn me off, Bert. I heard you the first time."

"Not well enough, I guess. Yeah, I heard about the pipe bomb. Dicky sent fragments to Madison, and we've been taking the note around to the university Art Department to see if they can identify somebody who prints like that. Don't get your hopes up. Probably anybody who has taken art can."

This dumb sheriff was a step ahead of me. "Any luck?" I asked.

"Not so far. We left a copy there and asked the department head to check with his faculty and students. Might get a lead that way."

"I take it seriously," I said.

"Like I said, we're looking into it."

"I came, actually, to bring you this." I handed him a copy of my copy of the secret page Polly Rector had given me.

"What the hell is this?" he said.

"It's German," I said.

"I know it's German," he said. "Where did you get it?"

"I can't tell you that."

"The hell you can't. This is a murder case. Are you impeding a murder investigation?"

"Not at all. That's why I brought you the page."

"Counselor, I can get a court order."

"In that event you'll have to explain to the court why this page is so important to a murder case. Maybe the CIA or the NSA or whatever it is would not be happy to have you making it public."

"What do you know about these papers?"

"I know that there were secret papers on the chancellor's conference table when his body was discovered. I know that someone removed them. I assume that was you or the Silvertown Police or the Feds, and that, in any event, you contacted the Feds and they told you to suppress any news about them. They have the papers."

The sheriff was nonplussed and furious. "Did you read this?" He held up the paper.

"Of course."

"How did you know about the papers?"

"Jim Fountain saw them when he and Hannah entered the office to find the body. Train's secretary said she saw no papers when she went to work on Monday."

"How did you know they were secret? Did Fountain look at them?"

"He says he just saw them on the table in disarray. He says he didn't know what they were."

"You haven't answered my question."

"That's a secret."

"You don't have secrets from me, Counselor."

"I've got lots of secrets from you."

"Not this one."

"Including this one."

"This is a federal matter."

"Fine. Let me talk to the Feds."

"You crazy? Why would you want to talk to the Feds?"

"To find out what connection there might be between the papers and the murder of Bill Train."

"I told you to stay out of this case."

"Other person or persons unknown have tried to tell me that, too."

"I'm going to get a court order and stop you." He looked as though he might pull his Colt from its holster and arrest me right there.

"Go right ahead, then maybe we can get this thing out in the open."

"There are federal laws protecting the secrecy of intelligence agencies, Counselor. You could be in big trouble."

"So it is true then that the papers were intelligence papers. Well, well. Was Train working for the CIA or the NSA?"

"I'm going to talk to the Feds about you, Fogarty."

"Good. Tell them I'd like to talk to them myself. I have some questions for them, like: Did they assassinate the chancellor? Was he assassinated by agents from another government? His wife would like to know."

"I'm going to give you that chance, Fogarty. You know about the papers. You read a page of secret material. You refuse to tell me where you got it. I think they might be interested in talking to you."

"Tell them it's mutual."

"In the meantime, mind your own business."

"In the meantime, I intend to mind my business."

He leaned back toward the phone as I left.

My next business was the Art Department. I was annoyed at myself for not having thought of trying the artistic lettering of my bomb threat on Matt Monroe.

Susie and I had bought several drawings from Matt, and we think of him as a friend. We have a drawing of the dunes at Cape Hatteras. We had camped at Hatteras several times when we were younger and Cathy was just a toddler. And we have a piece of his sculpture in rosewood on the fireplace mantel. Matt is from Texas and wears a cowboy hat with small Confederate flags in the band. He has achieved recognition for his work, but you'd never know it. He acts like a cornpone to people he doesn't like, or when he is shy. His wife is a tall, lovely Texas gal who nearly freezes to death every winter, but Matt likes the hunting and fishing and lack of pressure and refuses to leave beautiful northern Wisconsin.

Matt was in the foundry with his sculpture class, casting a bronze piece. He waved at me and continued to show the students how to pour the hot metal into a hole in the sand where a black wax figure was waiting to dissolve away and provide a shape for the bronze. He made the students stand back and he poured quickly and carefully. He maneuvered the pot back from the sand and gestured to his assistant to take over.

"Hey," Matt said. "I hear you've been getting bomb threats."

"That's what I'm here about."

"Come on in," he said, and led me to his office at the end of the foundry. His office looks like a factory as much as the foundry does, cluttered and full of clay dust. He wiped off a chair and invited me to sit down. He sat in his swivel chair and leaned back.

"You decided to mind your own business?"

"You know me better than that."

He laughed. "What business you been warned away from?"

"Hannah Train asked me to look into the murder of the chancellor."

"Oh lord!" he said. "He got killed with the sculpture I gave him."

"I know," I said.

"You gotta find whoever did it. Bill Train was a good man. He did a lot for this university. That foundry you were just in is only one thing he did. We wouldn't have it and a lot of other things, except for him."

"I'm looking. Have you seen the bomb threat note?"

"Yep."

"Who printed it?"

"I'm not sure."

"Who do you think did it?"

"Damnit, Sean, I hate to rat on anybody."

"Matt, the person who printed that could be connected with the murderer, may, in fact, be the murderer."

"I can't believe that. Teddy couldn't kill anybody."

"Teddy Hughes?"

"He can talk you to death, but he wouldn't hurt a fly. Besides, why would he want to kill the chancellor?"

"Why did he send me a bomb threat?"

"I don't know. It just doesn't figure."

"Is he here?"

"I don't think so. I think he took off early this morning after that guy from the sheriff's office brought over a copy of the note."

"Where's his office?"

"Up on the third floor."

"Has anyone told the sheriff's office about Teddy?"

"I don't think so."

"I'll go up and check his office."

"Don't tell him I told you, O.K.?"

"O.K. Thanks, Matt."

Matt shook his head sadly.

I climbed to the third floor and found Teddy Hughes's office. When I knocked, there was no answer. The door had a translucent window as its top panel. I thought I could see a shadow of a human figure in the light that came through it from the windows in the room beyond.

"Teddy?" I called.

I thought the shadow moved. I waited.

"It's Sean Fogarty," I said. "I want to talk to you."

The door opened a crack to a vertical slice of Teddy's face.

"What the hell do you want?"

"I want to know why you're trying to kill me."

He laughed in a high pitch and then got angry. His long, blond hair sagged over his ears in a beauty-shop wave; when he shook his head in pique, it whirled around his face.

"You're crazy," he said.

"One of us is," I said.

"Maybe somebody's trying to kill you because you lost another case for them." He worked up a sneer. He looked pale and a little shaky.

"I never lose a case," I said. "Why are you trying to warn me off?"

"Why should I want to warn you off?"

"That's my question."

"Maybe you're meddling in things you shouldn't."

99

"Now we're getting somewhere," I said. "Just what is it I'm supposed to be meddling in that I'm not supposed to be meddling in?"

He had backed into his office several feet. The door fully open now, I had advanced to make sure he didn't slam it in my face.

"How the hell should I know?"

"Then why did you send me the message?"

"What message?"

"The one in block letters, in your own inimitable printing."

"My printing is not unique."

"How can you say that? You are unique; your printing is unique, like your fingerprint."

"Like my fingerprint? What fingerprint?" Now he was worried. His smooth skin developed a small wrinkle between his plucked brows.

I advanced another two feet, and he backed into his desk.

"What did you have to do with the chancellor's murder?"

"I had nothing to do with the chancellor's murder."

"Then why are you throwing pipe bombs into my kitchen and tacking warning messages to the back door?"

"You can't prove I did any of that," he said.

"I think I can prove the note. Did somebody else make the bomb?"

He reached behind to the desk and brought around a metal letter opener and held it with the point in my direction.

"You're not going to prove anything," he said.

"From pipe bomb to letter opener," I said. "Not very sophisticated methods, truthfully." He had not been backing up because I was advancing; he had been planning all the while to arm himself.

"You leave me alone," he said, pointedly.

100

"You leave *me* alone," I said. I was no karate expert. How did one defend oneself against letter openers?

"Get out of my office."

"Can you prove you didn't kill the chancellor?"

"I don't have to prove it. And, in any case, I was in Chicago that Saturday."

"You can prove that?"

"I have witnesses."

"Who did, then? Are you protecting someone?"

"Who would I protect?"

"Your friend Polly Rector, perhaps?"

He sat down abruptly in his swivel chair, the letter opener now pointing toward the overhead light.

"She fought with him all the time, I understand," I said.

"She couldn't have done it," Teddy said weakly. "She was all broken up when it happened. That Sunday when I came back, she was having a crying fit all night. She said he was a spy for the CIA, that he was corrupt and evil."

"Then you do think she killed him?"

"I don't know. How should I know?"

"Is that why you warned me off?"

"Who said I tried to warn you off?"

"I did."

He brushed the hair out of his eyes. His eyes seemed cold and even amused. Maybe he did believe Polly did it. Maybe he didn't. But was that the reason he threw a bomb in my kitchen? He knew it would be hard to prove.

"This whole thing doesn't make sense," I said.

"You should mind your own damned business," he said.

"An exact quote," I said. He wasn't even trying to disguise the fact now. "Maybe I should take this whole thing to the sheriff."

"Screw the sheriff," Teddy said. "Get out." Then he laughed.

Maybe the sheriff would like that, I thought. And like

me to get out of his hair, too. Everybody wanted me out. What the hell was going on? There was nothing more to be gotten from Teddy in his present mood, but there was something queerer about him than his sexual preference. I waved and left, moving apace, lest he find it an opportunity to open up my back like a letter from mother.

# XVII

I went home for lunch. The snow in the street was dirty from cars. White Christmases are only when the snow is fresh; after a few hours it's business as usual. Susie was out having lunch with friends. She left a note listing what was available. I made a ham and asiago cheese sandwich with peperoncini on the side. And a glass of cold milk.

When I got back in my office, I dialed Rusty Yeats and asked him if he knew Steve Wallace's wife's maiden name. He said his wife might know, since she and Wallace's wife were friendly and went to the same church. He called back in four minutes with the name.

I called Peoria, Illinois, and asked for the Jameson residence. There were two Jamesons; I asked for both numbers. The first number I called got no answer. The second answered, and I asked for Mrs. Steven Wallace and told who was calling. Mrs. Steven Wallace came on the line. I asked if she had been in Silvertown on Saturday, the tenth of April. She said she had not; she had come to Peoria the first of April. I asked if she was sure, and she assured me she was. Why was I calling? I explained I was doing some checking and thanked her.

Seventeen minutes later I got a call from Steven Wallace, asking what the hell did I think I was doing?

"Checking on your story," I said.

"You got no right to bother my wife."

"You offered her as a witness that you were at home between twelve and two on April 10. She says she was in Peoria."

"So what? I say she was here."

"Perhaps her mother will say she was there."

"You get your damned nose outta my business," he shouted and hung up.

Maybe his wife was a communist, too. Probably not a lesbian.

Julie buzzed to say she still hadn't reached Professor Richards and that Dicky James was on the line.

"Thanks for watchdogging my place," I said. For some reason I didn't understand myself, I didn't want to tell him about Teddy.

"O.K.," Dicky said. "I've got something else for you, though. There's a white Camaro in the driveway on Hickory."

"Thanks," I said.

"You going over there?"

"You bet."

"I'll send a car over to back you up just in case."

I thanked him and took off for Hickory Street. I drove in slowly and parked directly behind the Camaro.

There were tracks in the snow on the rickety stairs. I rapped on the door. After a minute, the door opened a crack. That handsome black face appeared again.

"You again," she said.

"Yep," I said.

"He isn't here."

"That's what you said yesterday, but he was."

The door suddenly opened wide. "Get the hell outta here, whitey." That came from a male black with an Afro and sunglasses.

"You Nick Lee?" I said.

"So what?" he said. "Get the hell outta here."

"I need to talk to you," I said.

"I don't talk to no honky nobody," he said.

He pushed the young woman aside and pushed at me. "No need to get rough," I said. "I just want to ask you a few questions."

"Like what?"

"Like where were you on Saturday, the tenth of April."

"Right here, boy. Right here with my baby, wasn't I, baby?"

"That's right, Nicky," said the young woman from inside the room.

"See? Now get off this property."

"Anybody else see you at that time?" I said.

He grabbed my arm and pulled me inside the apartment. He let go. The room was dark, but I could make out the young woman who talked to me at the door and another young woman standing near a sofa. Then I felt a slam to my face, and I fell back over a chair. The chair went over with me, and my head banged on the floor. I could hear the women screaming at Nick. I heard him clattering down the stairs. My face hurt like hell. My mouth was bleeding. I managed to get up and go to the doorway. Nick was standing by his car yelling. The young woman he had called "baby" pushed by me and screamed at him, "You crazy, you crazy." I wasn't cut out to play Sam Spade, I thought.

Nick got in his car and ran it two feet toward the garage, which was all the space he had, then he backed into my four-wheel drive with a bang, then he ran forward. He was turning, little by little. He repeated the forward-backward movement until he could slip past the garage. He drove across the snow-covered back lawn and onto the back lawn of the house next door, through a small picket fence, and off onto the next street. I heard a police siren, brakes squealing, more siren, more squealing. I made my way down the stairs. The young woman was behind me. She said, "He's crazy, Mr. Fogarty. He threatened to kill us."

I could hear the siren still going, but it seemed stationary. There was no more squealing. I walked quickly to the street he had driven to. The young woman followed, saying, "Oh my God, oh my God." The police car, its lights flashing, was at the next intersection. Nick's car was on the sidewalk. Two policemen were grappling with him. People were coming out of houses. With "baby" in tow, I half-ran to the intersection, wiping the blood off my mouth with a Kleenex. By the time we got there, the police had Nick cuffed to the car door. He was yelling obscenities.

"You got nothing on me, you pigs," he yelled.

One policeman, young Fred Dawson, a little out of breath, said, "How about assault, trespass, vandalism, and resisting arrest, for beginners?" He knew the book. He was taking courses in criminal justice at the university, his father had informed me at Rotary.

"Baby" took my arm. "I'm sorry, oh my God. I'm sorry, Mr. Fogarty. I didn't mean to lie to you, but I had to. He was there yesterday, but I was scared."

"It's O.K.," I said. "I understand. What's your name?"

"Betty Ransom," she said.

Fred Dawson came over to me. "You O.K.?" he said. "Looks like you caught one."

"That I did," I said. "But I'm O.K."

"You'll be down to file charges?"

"You bet," I said. I felt my front teeth. They didn't wiggle, and that was a good sign.

The other policeman was on the radio, asking for a wrecker. Dawson walked to the car, and they put Nick inside the back and locked it. The crowd stood watching at a respectful distance. Mrs. Jackson was there and waved at me.

"Betty," I said. "Was Nick with you that Saturday, April 10 between twelve and two?"

"I'm scared," Betty said.

"I understand. But I don't think Nick will bother you again."

"We didn't want him staying with us. He just made us let him stay."

"I understand," I said.

"You don't understand," she said. "He can get us."

"We'll get him out of town," I said.

"He'll get us in Milwaukee, then," she said.

"Was he with you that Saturday?"

"He was in the morning. Mr. Fogarty, I'm scared to talk."

"Was he there between twelve and two?"

"Do I have to tell?"

"You might have to tell the court."

"No, sir. He was with us until about ten. He said he was going back to Milwaukee."

"Did he go to Milwaukee?"

"No, sir. He came back that night about six."

"Did he say where he had been?"

"He never told us anything. He just came and went as he pleased."

"You knew him when he was here as a student?"

"That's right. He was a big man because he was militant."

"You were his girlfriend?"

"I didn't want to be."

"What about the girl who shares your apartment?"

"She was his girlfriend, too. He made her be. She was scared, too."

"I'll try to help you," I said. "I'll get an injunction from the court. Call me tomorrow. Do you have a phone?"

She shook her head. "We use the pay phone at the Student Center."

"O.K., call me. I don't think Nick will be getting out very fast. I'll get the injunction as soon as I can, and we'll keep an eye on you, if and when he gets out."

She nodded her head. Nick started yelling at her from the closed police car.

"Keep your mouth shut, baby," he yelled. "I'll kill you."

I could understand why Betty was scared.

# XVIII

Professor Wilbur Richards, one-quarter American Indian, was waiting for me in my office. When I came in the reception area and headed for my suite, Julie (eyebrows up at the sight of my face) handed me a piece of paper with his name on it and nodded in the direction of a man sitting in a corner chair reading yesterday's *Silvertown Bee*.

I walked over to him. "Professor Richards?" I said.

"That's right," he said. "You're Fogarty?"

"Right. Please come in."

He led the way, and I pointed to a chair opposite my desk.

"Your secretary called me and said you wanted to see me," he said.

"I would have been happy to go to your office," I said.

"That's all right," he said. "I was coming downtown anyway, and I thought I might as well stop by."

Richards looked more like an Irishman than an American Indian. But of course some Irishmen look more like Indians than Irishmen. Richards was tall, light-skinned, with a prominent nose, buck teeth, dark hair. He was dressed in jeans and a wool checked shirt under a jean jacket, the attire of a northern Wisconsin Indian—or a northern Wisconsin whitey. It doesn't matter. We're democratic up here.

"Mr. Richards, if you'll excuse me for a minute, I need

109

to wash the blood off my face. I've just had a slight altercation with a descendant of General Lee."

"I thought that might not be the way you look normally," he said.

I went into my private WC and regarded my face in the mirror. My slightly ruddy face was slightly ruddier. Not quite as bad as I had thought. Susie would still recognize me. I was the same six-foot, middleweight, sandy-haired Irishman I was before. There was a swelling of the upper lip and a cut inside the lip and a bit of a cut in the cheek. I suspected Nick Lee had been wearing a ring. I felt the back of my head and found a small nodule. It could have been worse. I rinsed my face off in the lavabo with cold water. Not exactly handsome, but lots of character, right? Anyway Susie liked it.

When I returned, it looked as though Richards were trying to read the papers on my desk upside down. It couldn't have interested him very much. Contracts are deliberately turgid and full of legalese so that lawyers can make a living.

"What did you want to see me about?" Richards said.

"Mrs. Train has asked me to look into her husband's murder," I said.

"And you think *I* murdered him?"

"Did you?"

"In a way, I suppose. And he deserved it."

"What way was that?"

"I put an Indian spell on him."

"With a piece of sculpture?"

"With chants and dances."

"And it worked?"

"Seems to have."

"And he deserved it?"

"I think so."

"Why?"

"Because of his anti-Indian attitude, racial bias, white man's superiority."

"What makes you think he was biased?"

"I am the only Indian with a full-time position at Silvertown, and he fired me. This, mind you, in a region where there are more Indians than any other part of the state."

"He fired you because you are Indian."

"No question."

"I understood that the enrollment in your department was declining and a position had to be eliminated."

"That was not the real reason."

"I thought the department made the choice where a position was taken away."

"When the position was taken away, there was no doubt who they would pick."

"Is the department biased, too?"

"Their action speaks for itself."

"I understand you thought the chancellor should have been impeached?"

"I certainly did. He failed to uphold the law."

"Which law was that?"

"Laws about equal opportunity and affirmative action."

"Did you decide to impeach him, as it were, yourself?"

"I did, but the senate refused to oust him. They should have voted no confidence."

"I understand the chancellor worked very hard for equal opportunity and affirmative action. He appointed the first woman dean in the history of the university."

"Women don't need affirmative action. They're the majority, not a minority."

"In the population."

"Yeah. And the College of Education is full of them. I'm talking about Native Americans and blacks. Women rule this country. They haven't been subject to slavery and

111

genocide. Think about what the white men did to the Indian population of this continent. Don't you think you need to recompense the genocide that was committed by your forefathers?"

Through all of this he projected a lofty air, using his height, even when he was sitting down, the way a judge uses his raised bench.

"What kind of recompense?"

"Education, jobs, payment for the confiscation of our lands."

"And retribution?"

"That, too, where it is needed."

"As in the case of Chancellor Train?"

"He got his retribution, didn't he?"

"Just what he deserved?"

"Exactly."

"Who carried out the retribution?"

"I don't know, but I thank him as my brother."

"One of your brother Indians?"

"Could have been. That would have been just. Or one of my brother animals."

"Your brother animals?"

"Our spirits sometimes assume the form of animals."

"Does your spirit sometimes assume the form of an animal?"

"Sometimes I am a wolf." His eyes had begun to glaze over a little. Would he turn into a wolf before my eyes?

"Did you, in your form as a wolf, take your vengeance on the chancellor?"

"Not to my knowledge."

"You might have assumed the form of a wolf and done it?"

"That's possible, but I don't think so."

"Where were you that Saturday?"

"I was on the Lost Lake Reservation."

"Did you assume your animal form while you were on the reservation?"

"I don't think so."

"What were you doing on the reservation?"

"I was having beer and communing with my brothers."

"Which brothers?"

"My brother Indians."

"They would bear witness to your being there drinking beer and communing?"

"I am sure they would."

"What time did you go to the reservation?"

"I don't remember exactly."

"Morning, noon, afternoon, night?"

"Before noon, I think."

"You don't remember?"

"Not exactly. I don't wear a watch."

"Why not?"

"I don't believe in subjecting myself to the slavery of time."

"How do you get to class on time?"

"I read the sun. When I have classes, I listen to the bells."

"Did you read the sun on April 10?"

"There was no sun on April 10."

"You remember that well?"

"It was an important day."

"An important day?"

"An important day for Indians."

"Their chief enemy in the university suffered the consequences of his oppression?"

"Right."

"Carried out by an Indian?"

"It doesn't matter. Carried out, that's what matters."

"A dark day for the university."

"The sun came out that evening, a glorious sunset."

"To celebrate the death of the chancellor?"

"A sign of His approval."

"His approval for what?"

"For the action of the avengers."

"Who are the avengers?"

"My brothers."

"Who are your brothers?"

"My fellow victims of the white man's society."

"Did they avenge your oppression on the chancellor?"

"Whoever did it acted on our behalf. He is my brother."

"I thought you were three-quarters white."

"My soul is Indian."

"Professor Richards, can you shed any light on the murder of Chancellor Train?"

"I have shown you the light. If you have not seen it, it is because you are blind." He stood up, tall and solemn as a Baptist preacher. "And you, too, will feel the retribution which is to be wrecked upon the white man for the evils you have committed against us." He walked out, clomping on the wooden floors like the personification of drums on Judgment Day.

I sat at my desk for a few moments, trying to regain my sense of reality. A little more of Professor Richards, and I might float away in the form of a pigeon.

# XIX

I asked Julie to call Jim Fountain. She found him this time in his office.

"Jim, this is Sean Fogarty again."

"Yes, sir," he said.

"When you're on duty, I assume you walk around the campus from time to time?"

"That's right."

"On the Saturday the chancellor was murdered, did you walk down the mall, or observe it?"

"A number of times."

"Between the hours of, say, eleven and three, can you remember whom you might have seen on the mall or, for that matter, between the Administration Building and Kinkaid Hall?"

"I saw a couple of dozen people on the mall. I didn't see anybody between Administration and Kinkaid."

"Can you remember specially who you saw on the mall?"

"I didn't recognize everybody I saw. I remember seeing a few professors and students. There was Professor Monroe over by the Wall Memorial Art Building, and Professor Richards and Professor Jackson, and that lady dean from Education."

"You saw Professor Richards on the mall?"

"Yes."

"What time was that?"

"A little after eleven, I think."

"Anybody else?"

"Well, there were a lot of students, groups of them, going between the Student Center and the dorm complex."

"Did you notice any male black students?"

"Yeah, I sure did. Two of them."

"Did you recognize them?"

"Yeah, one was Nick Lee, and the other was Randy Jarrell."

"You know them?"

"Yes, sir. Nick is a big wheel with the blacks. He got expelled, but he's still around. And Randy is a pal of his."

"How do you happen to know them?"

"I make it my business to know potential troublemakers."

"What time was it when you saw them?"

"Just after lunch. Must have been about one."

"Whereabouts?"

"They were coming out of the Student Center and heading down the mall."

"Anybody else?"

"Yeah. I saw one well-dressed man I didn't recognize. I never saw him before. He was walking in front of the library."

"Well-dressed?"

"He was wearing a suit, you know, and an open trench-coat."

"How old was he?"

"In his thirties, I'd say."

"And you think you never saw him before."

"I know I didn't."

"Anybody else?"

"There was Mr. Hartpence. He went to his office in the Admin Building about nine-thirty, but he left about eleven."

"You make the rounds of the parking lots on Saturday?"

"Yeah. Not as often as we do on a weekday, but we do."

"Did you see any unusual cars or out-of-state plates?"

"Well, we usually have out-of-state plates. Lots of students keep their home-state registrations. Mostly from Michigan and Minnesota and Illinois. There were two cars in the visitors' lot, one from Illinois."

"What kind were they?"

"One was a white Camaro with Wisconsin plates, and the other was a dark blue Ford LTD with Illinois plates."

"You don't remember the license numbers."

"No. I don't look at those unless there's a violation."

"On the Saturday the chancellor was murdered, you were in the security office when the chancellor's wife called?"

"That's right."

"There was no one else there?"

"On Saturday afternoon, unless there's something going on like a football game, we run light. One security man until evening, then two or three, depending."

"And you got her call about when?"

"A little after two. I have it exactly in my report."

"You had been patrolling the mall before that?"

"I came back to the office about twelve to eat lunch and then went out again."

"Do you punch clocks on your rounds?"

"No, it's not like a watchman's rounds. We vary our timing and where we go, to be flexible."

"So you can be anywhere on campus at any time?"

"Right."

"Have you observed any drugs on campus?"

117

There was a pause. Then he said, "We're not supposed to talk to the public about that, but I guess it's all right for you to know. Yes, we've got a drug problem. Not a big one, but we've got one."

"What kind?"

"Mostly pot, but some pills."

"Cocaine?"

"Some hard drugs."

"Do you know who's dealing?"

"We have our suspicions. We work with the town police on that. The police have an undercover agent on campus. They've nabbed a couple of small-time dealers in town, but so far only four or five users on campus since I've been here. Of course, nearly all those who smoke pot sell it to their friends."

"Do you know the extent of hard drugs on campus?"

"The Silvertown Police do, and the sheriff, I guess."

"Faculty members?"

"Some, I guess."

"Know who?"

"Not for sure."

"Have any ideas about who the dealers are? Faculty members, for example?"

"Not for sure. I'd guess that goes on off campus, at home, parties, that sort of thing, whatever does go on. I don't go to faculty parties, so I wouldn't know."

"But the dealing might take place on campus."

"Could be."

"Student dealers?"

"The sheriff is onto at least one student dealer, I know."

"You know who it is?"

"Ask the sheriff."

"Okay. And thanks again for your help."

"Any time."

He had sounded perfectly open. But wasn't that the way you wanted to sound if you were engaged in precisely the kind of malfeasance you were being questioned about? This campus cop had killed a man, perhaps under contract. It was unreal. Or maybe I was living in an unreal world.

I did the paperwork on the injunction against Nick Lee and asked Julie to walk it over to the courthouse. When she returned, I put on my parka and headed for city hall. I filed the assault complaint with Sergeant Ulrich and asked to see Nick Lee.

Nick wasn't yelling anymore, but he was still in motion. His arms were going; his legs were going. Jerky motions. He was on something. Maybe he should be left to suffer withdrawal pangs for a day or so, so he would be willing to talk more readily. I'd try now, anyway. I figured I was running short of time, if I were to clear up some of the things I needed to.

"I want to talk to you, Nick," I said.

"Up yours," he said.

"You were in Silvertown on Saturday, April 10, right?"

"Says who?"

"Say several people, including Officer Fountain who saw you on campus about one o'clock."

"So what?" His shoulders tried a shrug but jerked instead.

"That was the day Chancellor Train was murdered."

"Well, goody," he said.

"The murder took place sometime between twelve and two."

"So?"

"You were seen on campus at that time."

"Yeah?"

"You had a motive to kill the chancellor," I said. I was getting tired of all these types with motives.

119

"Sure, the bastard expelled me."

"Did you kill him?"

"I woulda liked to, but I didn't. Look, honky, you wanna lay this on me cause I'm black, huh? Well, it won't work. I was with Randy Jarrell all day, from morning till dinner time."

"Anybody else see you that day?"

"Lots of people. O.K.?"

"Like who?"

"Betty Ransom."

"Who else?"

"I don't know. Some kids in the Multicultural Center. We was there playing cards."

"You know their names?"

"I don't know their names. Randy does." His legs were jumping up and down about an inch, one, then the other. He was sweating, though the jail was not exactly warm. I still had my parka on, opened. "Look, man," he went on. "I didn't kill that dude. I had reason to, but I didn't. You just want to lay this on me cause I'm black."

"Nick," I said. "I don't want to lay this on anyone. I want to find out who did do it. I sure as hell don't want to lay it on someone who didn't do it, because that would mean the person who did would go free. I don't want that to happen. Bill Train was my friend. He was a good chancellor and did what he thought was right for the university and everybody in it, including you. You might not agree that what he did to you was right, but you had been re-admitted several times already, and you were flunking courses right and left. He had no choice."

"Yeah? Well, screw him. And screw you. You don't want to do things any righter than he did."

"Because I'm white?"

"White is right, right?" He was back in form.

"You may not believe me, but I care about fairness and justice, and I know the law does not always provide justice, nor do lawyers always work for it. But it's the best thing we've got, a lot better than every man for himself with his own guns and knives and fists." I rubbed my lip.

Nick almost smiled, but then his arms started jerking. "Don't give me no speeches, honky. That's a lot of bullshit and you know it."

"I understand you were a leader among the campus blacks."

"Yeah, so what?"

"And that you used intimidation to establish your leadership."

"Yeah? Who told you that? Betty?"

"Using intimidation is cowardly, you know. If you've got the stuff, you don't need to frighten people into following you."

"What the hell is this? Sunday school? And what the hell are you a leader of? The Rotary Club, the Mooses?" He laughed and then jerked his back back involuntarily.

Good question, I thought. But, in fact, I didn't want to lead anything. Except a witness now and then. "I'm getting an injunction, a court order, that will prohibit you from entering Betty Ransom's apartment, or from molesting her in any way, on any occasion, anywhere. O.K.?"

"You think a piece of paper from a honky judge is going to scare me?" His knees jumped up then and his feet rattled on the floor like teeth chattering in the cold.

"Would you like to get out of here?"

"Yeah, man, I gotta get out."

"What are you on?"

"None of your damned business."

"You could be in here for a while, days, maybe a long time until you come to trial."

"Oh no, I won't. I put in a call to Randy. He's going to get a lawyer. I'm going to get out on bail."

"Providing more serious charges are not filed."

He took off his sunglasses and glared at me. "Shit," he said. "You try any funny stuff to keep me in here, I got friends who might split more than your lip."

# XX

On the way out of the police station, I stopped to catch Dicky James and asked him to delay releasing Lee on his bail, if it was forthcoming, until I could get my injunction. He agreed to the stall if necessary. I told him about Lee's motive and his claim to an alibi. He said he'd check it.

I had a feeling of things going along to some conclusion. I still had some questioning of suspects to do; I still had some checking of stories to do; I still had to face the Feds. My routine was beginning to pall on me. Was I really getting the information I wanted? Did I really have the ideas I had assured Susie I had? Intuition. I worked that way, but that was no good in court. Tactics, I said to myself. That was enough for the day.

The following day the snow had turned to slush in a cold rain. The Great Spirit was not celebrating. Spring is cruel in northern Wisconsin, because it promises and then recants and then promises and then recants and never does come. In June it is suddenly summer, with heat, humidity, and legendary mosquitoes.

Julie had already received the call. An unidentified person would arrive in my office at ten. I asked Ben Bosch to try for my injunction with Judge Pound at ten; if he got it, he should get it to the jail on time.

The unidentified Fed was on time. He identified himself

with a card, his picture in the corner. All of it probably an official alias. He was of medium height; he was of medium weight; he was medium in features; he wore a dark suit. Probably, I thought, he drives a Ford LTD.

He folded his wallet and returned it to his rear pants pocket, draped his trenchcoat over the back of a chair. "I understand," he said, "you have the missing original page of a secret document belonging to the federal government." He sat down.

"You do not understand correctly," I said. I sat down behind my old rosewood desk.

"You do not have it?"

"I do not. I have a copy of the page."

"Who has the original?"

"I don't know."

"Where did you get the copy?"

"It was given to me confidentially by a client." (Polly would, no doubt, be less than amused at my making her my client.)

"Your client stole the paper?"

"Not to my certain knowledge."

"You don't know where he got it?"

"I do not."

"That page belongs to the government and must be returned."

"I have a feeling it will be returned before long, but I cannot be sure."

"That's not good enough."

"A lot of things about this whole affair are not good enough."

He didn't like the sudden shift from his grilling and admonishing me to my offering a critical comment. His eyes became slits. He pursed his lips.

"The law with respect to classified material has apparently been broken by several individuals. There could be consequences." He was determined to keep his position.

"There have already been consequences to something or another, perhaps relating to your document and Chancellor Train's role, whatever it was, in regard to it. A good man, a man important to the university and the state, has been murdered. It has occurred to some of us that that relationship may indeed be a controlling factor in his murder."

He blinked. "The government did not murder Dr. Train, Mr. Fogarty. The document was incidental to the murder."

Aha. Now he was answering me. "You are confident, are you, that no agent of the United States government and no agent of any foreign government murdered Dr. Train or was involved in his murder in any way, and, further, that the document in question was not in any way connected with the murder?"

"That is correct."

"What were you doing on the University of Wisconsin—Silvertown campus on Saturday, April 10 of this year?"

There was a hairline crack in his composure. It took him a second to snap back. "I am not at liberty to concede that I was on the campus, or if I were, to reveal what I was doing."

"Oh, come off it, Agent Whatever Your Real Name Is. There are laws with respect to murder and any material witness to a murder—and, indeed, all facts with respect to a murder—and they are applicable to people who work for the government as well as to ordinary citizens."

The crack got wider. His face had taken on color that was not due to the modest heat that our central heating supplies to Clancy's Tavern, the Hideaway, and the law offices of Fogarty, Svensen and Bosch. He took a deep breath through his nose.

"Mr. Fogarty, you are out of line on this. We are dealing with a secret document that is essential to the defense of the country against its foreign enemies. Neither that document nor I nor any agent of the government had anything to do with the murder of Dr. Train."

"How can you be sure of that?"

"We are sure."

"The document was spread out in a messy way all over the conference table in the chancellor's office when the body was discovered. The papers were gone by Monday morning. One page was missing. Am I correct in assuming that you personally recovered the document?"

"The document was recovered, minus one page."

"The fact that it was strewn about the table in a way contrary to the way Chancellor Train was accustomed to work is interesting, is it not?"

He looked at me.

"And the fact that one page was missing is also interesting, is it not?"

He kept looking at me.

"Do you have an explanation for these facts?"

"I am not at liberty to say."

"Don't be such a pompous ass, Mr. Agent. We are dealing with a murder. The connection comes right here. It is very likely that the person who murdered the chancellor messed up the papers on his table and took the missing page, right?"

"That's your assumption."

"Damn right it's my assumption. And, further, it is my assumption that a) the murder took place because the murderer wanted something either from that document or perhaps another document or documents also secret and possibly now missing in its/their entirety, or b) the murderer, having killed the chancellor, discovered the document by chance, messed it up in perusing it, took a page for his own purpose and skipped."

126

"I'm not at liberty to comment on your assumptions."

"Why do you persist in being a pompous ass? Would you rather answer in court?"

"We do not have to reveal intelligence secrets in court."

"Ho ho. Tell me, did Train work for you?"

"I can't answer that."

"Was he a consultant? Were the documents stolen? Was he an enemy agent?"

"I can't answer those questions."

"Let me try some scenarios on you. One: Train worked as a consultant for your agency. He had been in intelligence after World War II. He was an expert on Germany. He even ran agents in East Germany. You used him occasionally to evaluate information about East Germany, or to identify names or activities."

His face was distinctly red by now and was set and immobile. "The second scenario: He was captured in East Germany on one of his trips to visit some of his agents. He was wounded, tortured, and turned. He continued to work for the East Germans as they required."

His face was still set.

"The third scenario: Both scenarios are true."

"Fogarty," he said, "you're out of your tree."

My God, he was human, after all. Even a faint accent came through. Southern Virginia, or Tennessee. (Accent on the first syllable.)

"Do you know Laurence and Bella Leiberman?"

His eyes flickered, but no answer came forth.

"Have you terminated anybody lately 'with extreme prejudice'?"

If his steely-eyed silence was meant to answer me, I was convinced.

"Do you speak German?" I said.

"I'm not on the witness stand, Fogarty."

"True enough," I conceded. "I get carried away sometimes. Anyway, I think I know what I needed to know. How about you?"

He looked almost dumfounded. "I don't have the information I have to have."

"You don't need it. And I am not at liberty to tell you. I will tell you this much. At this point probably only two or three or four of Silvertown's citizens have seen that missing page of reports on anti-state activity in Leipzig, and they couldn't care less what it actually says. And what it does say is not vital to the defense of the United States, though it is possible that something in it might be of use to those who analyze the state of affairs in East Germany. What the person or persons who have read that page care about is that their chancellor may have been doing some work for the intelligence service of the government. Some may take a dim view of that. Others may be flattered that their chancellor was such an expert that he could contribute to the intelligence effort of the government to learn more about a satellite of the Soviet Union. The only thing you have to worry about is whether we think that's all there is to it. If that's all there is to it, fine and dandy. A coincidence to murder. If we don't believe that's all there is to it, there may be hell to pay. You have your copy of the page. Take it and go. If I find the original, I'll mail it to you."

The agent rose, his face at its reddest. "You will be hearing from us, Fogarty."

"Do you like to hunt?" I said. "Lots of hunting up here. We're pretty good at it. We thin out the deer herd real good. Come back, and we'll get the boys together, and we'll show you a real good time in the woods."

He picked up his trenchcoat and walked out.

# XXI

Maybe I had been a bit brisk with the gummit agent. I might even get sent to Siberia. But I was already in Siberia. I decided not to worry. If scenario two or three were true, I'd hear something. If number one were true, I'd hear not another word. I dialed Betty Olson and said I'd be in to look at the nasty alumnus letter, and I asked if I could see Acting Chancellor Hartpence at the same time. Two ducks in one pond. Betty called back and said I could if I came now. I went now.

The door to Hartpence's office was open, and he waved me in before I could look at the letter that Betty was about to hand me. Acting as chancellor had given Hartpence a lift. He was beaming under his Moe haircut and was wearing a sport coat and slacks instead of his usual jeans and old sweater. Still had on his trusty old cowboy boots.

"I hear you're stirring things up, as usual," he said cheerfully.

"You can tell more about people when they dance," I said, "than when they sit."

He laughed dutifully. "Any progress?"

"Some."

"How can I help you?"

That was a new tone. He had been stingy with his help on the phone from Madison, when I wanted to look at the mail. "I'd like to see that nasty letter, of course."

"Bill got a slew of them right after Pickel was returned to teaching," he said. He buzzed Betty. "Bring the letter from Principal Bob Warren in. The counselor can read it in here."

"Principal?" I said.

"Yeah. He's the one who wrote the nastiest letter. He organized a group of Pickel's former students, most of them coaches or principals."

Betty handed me the handwritten letter. What I read was the following:

Chancellor William S. Train
Silvertown University
Silvertown, WI

Dear Sir:

You have done a bad thing for atheletics in the state. and you done a bad thing to our beloved coach Pickel. He was an inspiration to generations of physical education students at Silvertown University. You are the one should be releeved of your dutys. You wont get away with this.

Sincerely,
ROBERT WARREN, Principal
Oak Creek High School

"That," I said, "is one of your graduates?"

Hartpence smiled ironically. "Phys ed," he said. "We have higher standards now than we had twenty years ago, when Bob Warren was here, but they come to us illiterate from the high school too frequently, and they sometimes get by illiterate after they pass composition with a D. There is no requirement that they be literate or demonstrate lit-

130

eracy to graduate. Bill tried for fifteen years to get such a requirement through the Curriculum Committee, but he was blocked each time by the English Department—they didn't want the extra work; the program was O.K. as it was—and other faculty who didn't want more credits or time spent in English to the detriment of their own programs."

"The English Department can stop the chancellor from making sure the students are literate when they graduate?"

"The faculty controls the graduation requirements."

"Why am I not more illiterate than I am?"

"You came from a literate family. You majored in English. You went to law school. It's a matter of chance."

"That's dumfounding."

"It's not all that uncommon in American education now."

"And a school principal?"

"It happens often enough that successful and popular coaches are made principals."

"Why, for God's sake?"

"That's what the community wants. Schools exist in part—in too much a part—to provide sports entertainment for the community, parents, and alumni. Natural enough, then, that when a popular figure wants to step up to an easier and higher-paying job he takes a few easy courses at the university, qualifies, and is chosen by the school board—composed, remember, of community people, parents, and alumni."

"I'm going to talk to Seamus Heaney, superintendent of Public Instruction. He's an old friend."

"Seamus is trying his damnedest. We've all talked with him. He's a member of the Board of Regents, too, by virtue of his office, and he's been on the backs of the chancellors to set higher standards. But he suffers and the chancellors suffer from political resistance. And the legislature is tired of sinking more and more tax dollars into

131

special programs that show very little. They say, why should they fund the university to teach students what they have already funded elementary schools to do? Seamus says, until the university sets higher admissions and graduation standards, he can't get the schools to do better. It's all political, and it comes back to parents and communities."

"Whoof," I said. "Well, that's not why I came to see you here, but I'm going to think about that one. Let's get back to this group of alumni you say illiterate Bob Warren set up. What did they do?"

"They went to the university system president and complained, asking him to fire or at least overrule the chancellor."

"What happened with that?"

"The president told them that personnel decisions of that sort were entirely within the prerogative of the chancellors. He didn't interfere. There were rules of procedure and that Bill had followed the rules and his prerogatives."

"Did they try anything more?"

"I don't really know."

"Would they have been mad enough, if they couldn't have his head, to bash it in?"

"Mad enough, maybe, but it's hard to believe they would go as far as that."

"Somebody did."

"That's true. And some of those ex-jocks are stupid enough, I suppose. Still, that seems a bit much."

"Is Warren still principal at Oak Creek High?"

"You bet. In fact he called me yesterday afternoon."

"He called you?"

"Yes." Hartpence laughed. "He wanted to know if I was going to restore Pickel to the football coaching job."

"I'll be damned," I said.

"I told him we had a new coach and he was going to

stay on the job. It's funny, because we all took part in the decision to ask Pickel to step down. It was unanimous."

"Warren expected that once Bill was out of the way Pickel would get his coaching rank back?"

"So it seems."

"May I have a copy of this?"

He hesitated, then agreed. He buzzed Betty and asked her to come and get the letter and copy it.

"What can you tell me about the Leibermans?"

"Laurence and Bella? They teach in the Language Department. Laurence teaches German; Bella, who originally came from Russia, teaches Russian, one class. Not much demand for Russian at Silvertown. They're both on leave this semester."

"They're not in town?"

"No, Laurence is in New York, and Bella went to Israel to visit her daughter."

"Did Bill bring them here?"

"I guess, in a way. They were recommended by a friend of Bill's in the State Department. They were highly educated refugees from East Germany, and they needed help in relocating and finding work. He had taught in some university there, but was being harassed because he was a Jew. We were looking for somebody to teach German. We added the Russian, since Bella was available and we could hire her part-time."

"Bill didn't know them before?"

"Not that I know of. I don't think so."

"And they're both away."

"That's right."

"Where were you on that Saturday?" I said.

Hartpence looked surprised. "I came to my office for a short time in the morning. I had some things to get ready for an executive council meeting on Monday morning. I left about ten-thirty or so. I went home and worked on a book I've been trying to write for the past ten years. My wife was there. Do I need a witness?"

"We have to examine everybody's opportunity."

"I suppose so." He looked thoughtful.

"I heard a story that your first wife died under mysterious circumstances, I guess that's the phrase. Silvertown gossip."

"It's true," he said. He began to fiddle with the long wooden letter opener on the desk. It had an elaborate handle with a carving of some sort. "The medical examiners were never able to determine the cause of death."

"What were the circumstances?"

"I came home from teaching—this was at a small college in North Carolina—and found her dead in her bed. She had been asleep when I left early in the morning for my first class. I could hear her snoring a little. When I got back at noon she was dead."

"There was never any suspicion that you might have killed her somehow?"

"Of course there was suspicion, since the cause of death couldn't be determined, but I had been in class or in my office with students all morning."

"The police questioned the students?"

"Yes, they did. They knew I was very fond of my wife. She was Polish. I met her when I was in Warsaw on a Fulbright. She was difficult, temperamental sometimes, but that was part of her charm."

"And the time of death was established as sometime while you were at school?"

He nodded.

"So it was left as causes unknown?"

"That's true." He caressed the carved handle of the paper cutter. "I left the college because of it. Even though I couldn't have killed my wife, there was always some doubt. I've never tried to hide the facts about her death. When I

134

came here, I told the committee and the chancellor."

"You got along well with Bill?"

"Very well. We saw eye to eye about almost everything."

"You now have an opportunity for the chancellorship, I suppose." Why did people fiddle with paper knives in my presence?

"Possibly, but that's up to a search-and-screen committee of faculty and students and then the president and the Regents."

"That's a beautiful paper knife," I said.

He was startled and dropped it. "Yes," he said. "It's from Africa."

His intercom buzzed. Betty told him he had a call from Madison. I thanked him and said I would be going. He waved and picked up the phone.

Betty had the copy of Warren's illiterate letter for me. She handed me a little note with it. "Open it later," she said softly. She looked a little frightened.

I opened it when I got to my car. It said, "Please call me at home after work when you can. I have something more for you."

# XXII

"There's nothing for it but to go to Madison," I said. "I'll fly down on the afternoon plane and rent a car and drive to Oak Creek. Warren said he'd see me first thing in the morning at nine. I'd like to see President Joyce too, if I can. I have asked Julie to see if he could fit me in sometime during the day. That means I don't know when I'll get back. I'll call."

Susie had been out attending a P.E.O. gathering (a kind of uppity women's club. Susie had never forgiven me for telling her what those letters spelled in Spanish) when I went home for lunch. I called her from the office and reached her just before I left for the plane. She was not happy.

"This thing is taking you away from your work, and it's scarier and dirtier than I thought it would be. It seems to come off on us, on Silvertown."

"It was your idea. And you can't dig without getting into some dirt. The dirt is there."

"I know. I just wish I hadn't suggested it. The ladies were talking about it at the meeting. Everybody just wants this thing settled so we can get back to normal."

"Normal?" I laughed. "You want me to quit?"

She hesitated. "I don't know. Are you close?"

"Things keep cropping up. I may have been wrong in

some of my first ideas. I'm not sure yet. I have to cover all the bases."

"Did you forget about the benefit concert at the university tonight?"

"Damn."

"It's the chamber group. They're doing the Sonata in C Minor for Oboe and Continuo."

I hesitated. The university chamber music group is pretty good, and Handel is even better. Then the old Irish Catholic work ethic took over. I would forgo the pleasure of Handel and dig my potatoes in Madison. "I have to go," I said. "I've already made the appointment, and I've got to get this done."

"Call me and be careful."

"I will. Love you."

"Love you."

I had packed my bag at lunchtime. Julie had called Betty Olson to say I'd see her the next day or so. Bosch had gotten a temporary injunction from Judge Pound. Lee had been warned before he got out on bail. Betty Ransom had called, and I told her we had the injunction and she should notify the police if Nick tried to move back in with her or molested her in any way. Lee had been warned, too, not to leave town. He had to find another place to live; probably Randy would put him up. And he had to find some of whatever it was he was on. There had to be a source in Silvertown.

I asked Dicky to find out whether any of our characters had a past on a police blotter somewhere. He said he'd try, but that was a tall request without much in the way of places to go on. He'd call Rusty Yeats and see if he could get some background place names.

Wisconsin Wings is a sort of airline. It flies a funny looking thing called "Shorts" that looks like a fat chicken with its wings clipped. It rattles and shakes and leaks cold air into the cabin, where two aisles of green-faced passengers cross themselves and hang onto their seat belts. It overflies Silvertown when there is snow on the ground. That's about every third day. But when it does run, it's faster than driving all that way in unstable spring weather.

Madison is beautiful from the air, especially in the summer, a neck of land between two lakes, and the university at the end of State Street going west and over the hill and beyond. In the winter the colors are drab, and the lakes are rough, white, empty spaces. The water doesn't break up until May sometimes. It's the rape capitol of Wisconsin. I discouraged Cathy from going there. (She didn't want to go there anyway, because she wanted to go East.) The capitol building sits in the middle of the neck like a carbuncle. Still, it's a stirring sight for a country boy like me. And I had good memories of going to law school.

It was dusk by the time I got to the Inn on the Park, otherwise known as the Park Motor Hotel. It takes longer to get your bag at the Madison airport than it does to fly there from Minneapolis, or even Chicago. I had my carry-on and rented a Toyota at the terminal.

I could catch a glimpse of the lit-up capitol from my window and had a good view of an old building leased by the Department of Corrections across the way. And the bare branches of trees that adorn the square. I went to the restaurant at the Top of the Park for a Dewar's on the rocks and a light supper. The Top of the Park is higher in quality than Jolly's. Its prices are also more elevated.

From the high windows of the Top of the Park, you can see the capitol dome with its golden angel top, suffused with light from spots. My father had served in the senate for one term in the forties. He had taken me as a kid into the rotunda, and I was awed speechless by all the space and height and the wide staircases and white marble. I sat at his desk while a debate went on. The confusion of people

138

coming and going and consulting in the midst of the debate made everything unintelligible but exciting. It was my father's view that a citizen had to do his duty. One term was enough of a duty. The legislature now is packed with young lawyers who seem not to be able to make a living in a law office.

I had a hard time sleeping. I always do without Susie. I'm a creature of habit. And clear affections and dislikes. (Because my work often consists of elucidating ambiguities?) I thought about my inquiries and the people and sorted out my reactions, tested my intuitions. There were still puzzles, in the people and their actions, in the motives. Was there an answer in this town, or someone who knew the answer? I tried to sleep and kept waking to the shadows of bare trees across my ceiling and the vision of the barren life of someone who could kill a good man. The absolute stop we all come to he came to much too early and undeservedly. When you get to a certain age, you think about the end. Concretely. How do you measure what it was all worth, especially when you are not given the chance? Would it actually be better that way?

The morning was gray, too. The coffee was not made from freshly ground beans. The pancakes in the coffee shop were cold when I got them. The air outside was cold. I rolled up the window and turned on the heater and drove in the morning traffic toward Oak Creek.

The high school looked like a high school. A consolidated school in a small town that brought in most of its students on buses from the small towns and farms. It was a dark enough day to have lights on in the classrooms.

Robert Warren resembled an ex-coach playing principal. His office smelled like a gym. He was big, going to fat, loud. He tried to be hearty, but when a lawyer asks you for an interview, you worry. You have a right to worry.

The customary social niceties seemed unnecessary.

"I understand you and your friends, former students of Coach Pickel, tried to get Train fired as chancellor," I began.

"Where did you get that?"

"From an authoritative source."

"Yeah, well, that's right. We did. He destroyed the reputation of a fine man, the best coach I've ever knowed."

"Destroyed his reputation?"

"That's right."

"I thought the chancellor merely asked him to relinquish his post as coach and go back to teaching."

"He shoulda been allowed to be coach as long as he wanted."

"You mean the coach should make the decision about his own tenure, that the chancellor has nothing to do with it?"

"Who the hell is a chancellor? That coach meant a lot to us."

"To whom?"

"To us. To us football players at Silvertown. We kept in touch all those years. We had reunions. He was an inspiration to us."

No doubt as beefy then as he was now, what had he played? Tackle? Fullback? I didn't want to ask.

"And you resented it when he retired to teaching after all those years?" I said.

"That's right."

"And you went to the system president to try to get the chancellor fired."

"Yeah. The son of a bitch shoulda been fired. We went to some Regents and to some legislators, too."

"With no results."

"Yeah, well, they was sympathetic, but they couldn't do nothin'."

"What else did you do?"

140

"We organized a letter-writing campaign to the papers, to the Silvertown paper and the Madison papers."

"With no results."

"Yeah. Well, they finally stopped printing them."

"What did you do then?"

"We tried to get the faculty to help us."

"Did they help you?"

"A couple. Green and Professor Rector and some others."

"Professor Rector helped you?"

"Yeah. She said it was very unfair. She said Pickel was an asshole, but he was being treated unfairly."

"She said Pickel was an asshole?"

"Yeah, well, she's kinda funny."

"So that didn't work?"

"Yeah."

"Then what did you do?"

"Nothin'."

"You didn't go bash his head in?"

"*I* didn't, no."

"Who did?"

"I don't know."

"One of your group?"

"Naw. They wouldn't do that."

"Some pretty tough cookies in your group, I would think."

"Yeah, that's right."

"They were pretty mad."

"That's right, but none of them would do a thing like that. They'd talked about roughing him up, but nobody would kill him."

"They talked about roughing him up?" Pickel had taught them that?

"Yeah."

"Maybe one of them did it without your knowing."

"Could be, but I don't think so."

"You called Acting Chancellor Hartpence to ask if he was going to reinstate Pickel in his old job?"

Warren was surprised. "Yeah."

"Train's body was hardly in its grave."

"We waited a week."

"After you got rid of him."

"After he was buried."

"So that didn't work either."

"We're still working on it."

"You're still working on it?"

"Yeah, we're going to start another letter campaign. We're still carrying the ball for Coach Pickel."

"Thank you for your time, Mr. Warren," I said, and stood up.

"You bet," Principal Warren said.

# XXIII

Back in Madison, I called Julie. My appointment was for one. That meant I could catch the afternoon plane with time to spare. I parked on Lake Street in the ramp and walked along State Street. It is now a kind of mall, all gussied up with bricks and benches and trees. The shops are the same as they had been in my student days: sandwich shops, bookstores, clothing stores, record stores—with different names and different owners, no doubt. I browsed in a bookstore, ate a corned beef sandwich at the Upstairs Downstairs. I bought some French roast coffee beans for Susie. I walked to the west end of State and puffed up over the hill past Bascom and walked down to Van Hise Hall. The offices of the University of Wisconsin System are located on the top floors of Van Hise. You might well be going into the executive offices of an insurance corporation.

President Joyce is tall, slightly bent, with dandruff on his shoulders and glasses sliding down his nose—another lawyer. They're everywhere. Given the increasingly litigious nature of our society, perhaps it's just as well that lawyers are occupying more positions outside law offices. We can sue each other without bothering the ordinary citizen.

President Joyce was coolly cordial. Julie had explained

what I was about when she made the appointment. He expressed his condolences again through me to Hannah (he had expressed them directly at the funeral). With fifteen years of service, Bill had been "an old timer," and he had appreciated his wise counsel on many occasions. The Regents had had great respect for, and confidence in, Bill. (And the president, not? Bill had been a bit too much his own person, I suspected. Joyce was rumored to like his own people in key positions. He was moving people and taking advantage of attrition to put them there. If you like empires, I guess you have to build your own.)

"It's highly unlikely," I said, "that Bill would have enemies in the system or the legislature or in Madison of a sort that would want to do him in physically, but I have to explore all hints of possible motives. The battles in the system with politicians, the competition among chancellors are, I am sure, largely verbal."

"They sometimes reach high levels of heat and low levels of language," Joyce said, "but I haven't observed any physical expressions of animosity. I can't imagine anyone at all wanting to murder him."

"I understand that a group of phys ed alumni from Silvertown visited you a year or so ago, asking for Bill's removal because he had relieved a football coach of his coaching duties."

Joyce laughed. "That's true," he said. "I explained how those things work, but they were not entirely satisfied, I think. They sent in letters as well."

"There was never any question, I assume, of you or the board taking any action about it."

"None whatsoever. It was all perfectly legal and proper."

"Do you know whether Bill did any consulting?"

"Not that I know of. He may well have, but he didn't mention any to me. He served on several state commissions, of course, and educational boards. He was serving on the State Crime Commission this year."

"The State Crime Commission? That's the new commission set up by the legislature?"

"Newly reorganized, I think, is more accurate. There was a commission that had been established some years ago, but it had not been very effective, and there was some contention between the legislature and the governor's office over its purpose, its scope, and reporting. The new commission was just started this year."

"Does the commission deal with organized crime?"

"I think it was intended to deal with all kinds of crime, including the problem of organized crime, drugs, and so on. Bill was particularly interested in providing educational opportunities to prisoners to reduce recidivism. He supported the PREP program, which offers university credit courses to prisoners. The hope is, of course, that, if the inmates can get some kind of education in prison, they will be encouraged to continue their education when they get out and find occupations other than the ones which got them in."

"You mean move up to white-collar crime?"

Joyce laughed. "Well, it does pay more, and you are less likely to be put in jail for it."

"Is it possible that his work on the commission has some connection with his violent death?"

"I hadn't thought about that. I doubt it, knowing how these commissions work, but you might want to contact Jane Ayre, who is chair of the commission. She would not want to reveal any confidential information they may have developed, but she would know at least if there is any possible relationship."

We chatted on a bit about this and that. He had his secretary find me a phone number for Ayre and a phone

145

to call from. Mrs. Ayre said she could see me that afternoon when she went in to the office to work with the executive director of the commission.

I climbed back over the hill and down to Lake Street, picked up my rented Toyota, and made for the square again on University.

Jane Ayre had white hair, looked matronly, and was sharp as hell. I explained my mission. She praised Bill and mourned his death.

"And you think there might be a connection between his terrible death and what we have been working on in the commission?" she said.

"That did enter my head."

"We're dealing with a broad spectrum of criminal activity," she said. "I can't think of any particular aspect of our inquiry that would have caused someone to murder him. What I mean to say is, we have not yet gotten down to singling out very many individuals who are known to be involved in so-called organized crime or drug-dealing and so on. We are undertaking studies of the various criminal activities going on in the state to see whether we can devise a better strategy for dealing with them. I should say that we have studied the illicit drug traffic as our first priority."

"Does the drug pipeline go to Silvertown?"

"It goes everywhere, including Silvertown."

"Did Bill have any special knowledge of the drug traffic, or knowledge of a sort that other members don't have of individuals involved in it? Would it be advantageous, in short, for any person or illegal business to have him out of the way?"

She thought for a minute. "I can't see why it would be advantageous to have Bill out of the way, any more than it would to have anyone else out of the way. Unless, of course, they intend to eliminate us one by one." She smiled.

It would be hard to believe anyone would want to harm Jane Ayre. But then I had thought the same of Bill until I met all the strange people on my list of suspects.

"Have any members of the commission received threats?"

She hesitated. "Not directly."

"Indirectly?"

"I suppose you could say so. You realize that we are, at least at this point, a kind of study group. We are authorized to take testimony and bring specific information to the attorney general or other law enforcement agencies, but we are not formally a prosecuting agency ourselves. Our main task is to make recommendations to the governor and legislature. As we uncover information, we may indeed be seen as threatening to some crime group or another."

"Could Bill's murder be interpreted as a warning to the commission?"

"If he was killed by a crime group, I suppose so, but we don't know that, do we? I would think we would have received some message calling our attention to his murder and suggesting that the same could happen to others of us."

"And you have received no such warning?"

"None whatsoever. Or perhaps I should say *I* haven't, and no other member of the commission has indicated that he or she has received such a warning."

"So it is not absolutely clear that this is not a potential explanation."

"I guess you're right. It is not absolutely clear. I shall question other members of the commission about that. No one has resigned, however, and no one has seemed less determined."

"Is there anything you can tell me that is, say, general knowledge anyway that I might not know, not being up on these matters. I am looking for background information

147

about the drug business. That is not to say I am aware of any connection between the chancellor's murder and the drug scene, but you have indicated that drugs get to Silvertown, and I have discovered that persons having to do with drugs have ties of one sort or another to the campus."

She put on a thoughtful look. "There are some things which are apparently generally known, at least by police departments, and newspaper reporters, and politicians, that I might outline briefly for you, at least as far as they might pertain to Silvertown."

She took a deep breath, then plunged ahead. "The so-called Mafia in Milwaukee, generally conceded to be run by the DiMarinis family, has reached into most parts of the state with their organization. They distribute hard drugs, among other activities. There is a rival organization, called the 'Black Mafia' familiarly, that also distributes drugs and is in competition with the DiMarinis group. That competition is frequently violent and is carried on in an increasing number of cities in the state. I have no specific information about Silvertown, except that it is no less victimized by the same problems. Chancellor Train, of course, knew all I'm telling you. If he was aware of any local connections to the drug mafias, he did not reveal his information to the commission, as I am certain he would have done. Does that help?"

"Very much. One more thing, if I may."

"Please."

"Could there be a leak from the commission to criminal groups?"

"You're convincing me that anything is possible, Mr. Fogarty."

"I don't mean to alarm you. I am simply trying everything on for size."

"I hope that one, at least, doesn't fit. In any case, I shall think about the questions you have raised, and if anything

148

seems to relate to Bill's death, I will most assuredly let you know."

As I thanked her and prepared to take my leave, she smiled at me like Helen Hayes and said, "Were I ever to commit a crime, I would think to commit it outside your bailiwick."

I laughed. "If you ever commit a crime, I'll gallop to your defense. I'm sure I could get you off without even having to present a case."

# XXIV

A sea of pines, white ponds like sails, the town compact with its first lights on, the sun at the crack of the horizon, out for a brief moment under the gray clouds: Silvertown. The plane rattled to a slippery stop. The wind was blowing, but I didn't care. I drove for home. It took me longer than I anticipated.

Though I was the only passenger debarking at Silvertown, I noticed another car starting up from the small airport parking lot and following me onto the highway. The airport is about five miles from town (allowing, no doubt, for a hundredfold expansion of the population), and for the first two miles the car following kept the same steady sixty miles per hour I was driving. As we began the slope down to Lost River, my follower speeded up and pulled out to pass. My alarm synapses were firing, and I took a firm grip on the wheel. The passing car swerved in front of me, striking the left front fender and forcing me to brake and pull toward the right shoulder. At this point in the slope to the river, I remembered as I went, there is no shoulder, and I flipped into the ditch, skidding in the mud with sounds of metal stress and the engine running wild. My car was now upside down, and I hung head down, observing quasars and black holes. I breathed hard and tried to recapture my senses. Was I hurt? I didn't think so. What about exploding gas tanks and all that? I managed with considerable difficulty to extricate myself from the trap of all the belts, turned off the ignition, opened the door with a hard push and crawled out.

I saw by stationary carlights that my pursuer, or someone, had parked on the highway ahead of me. I crawled up the ditch away from the road and struggled blindly into the brush. I heard voices and stopped to listen, crouching in the dead leaves.

"He ain't here," a voice shouted up from my wrecked car.

"He's gotta be," another voice shouted. I recognized the second voice. It belonged to Security Officer James Fountain, ex-hitman from Beloit. I breathed as quietly as I could. Fountain must have climbed down to the car, for the voices diminished in volume. I heard thrashing in the brush. I scrunched even lower and stopped breathing altogether.

"The son of a bitch must have run off," Fountain said, not ten feet from where my face lay burrowed into the cold mud.

"Iffin we don't have no lights, we'll never find him in this shit," his companion said. "What are we goin' to do 'bout his car?"

I could hear them clomping back toward the car.

"We'll just leave it," Fountain said. "We'll get him right next time."

I raised my head and peeked through the trees and dead weeds. They were scrambling up the ditch in the still burning headlight glare of my car. Fountain's companion looked very much like Deputy Fessler, Anderson's sidekick. Now that was interesting. They reached their car and drove off, but I stayed put, lest their departure be a ruse to catch me out on the highway.

In due time I returned to my car, turned off the headlights, climbed up the ditch to the highway, and started painfully toward town. Had they intended to set fire to my car with me trapped inside?

Three pickup trucks and a flatbed later, a VW bus approached from town, stopped beyond me and turned around. It was Matt Monroe's old camper. It came up beside me.

"Is that you, Sean? Jesus, what happened to you?" Matt opened the big sliding door and hopped out.

"Just coon hunting," I said.

"No decent coon would open his eyes in the dark with you looking like that," he said.

"I guess I do look a little bedraggled," I said.

He helped me into the bus and drove me home. I explained that my car had flipped over, and I was surely glad to see him. He was glad he came along.

And I was even gladder to see Susie, who was alarmed to see me. I gave her my flip story until after I had taken a shower and changed clothes. Then I gave her the longer version with Dewar's on the rocks about Fountain and Fessler.

Susie was duly stunned by my story. "Why, in heaven's name, would Bert Anderson or Jim Fountain or Fessler want to kill you?"

I told her then what I had learned from Jane Ayre. "I think," I concluded, "that I have stumbled on a nest of rattlesnakes. When I contacted the police chief in Beloit, I was walking blindly through the woods, and what he told me somehow got back to Fountain, or perhaps Anderson. Now we know whose woods these are."

"Be serious, Sean. Do you mean that our sheriff is linked to the Mafia?" She was aghast.

"He warned me off, remember? And Teddy warned me off with his pipe bomb and neatly printed explicit note. I suppose Teddy could have a separate reason, but I don't think so now."

"And Nick Lee works for the rival Black Mafia?"

"By Jove, you've got it."

"And what does all that have to do with Bill's murder?"

"I don't know. I thought I had the murder figured out, but now I'm up a tree with the snakes after me. Do snakes climb trees? Or am I mixing metaphors?"

"I wish you weren't mixed up in this at all."

"I'm more mixed up than my metaphors at this point, but I'm committed. I know what I know and they know I know. I have no choice."

"What are you going to do?"

"I don't know that either, but I'm thinking."

Susie made a quiche, and we ate quietly and went to bed and hugged each other for a long time.

# XXV

English muffins and more bad news. Julie called me at breakfast to tell me Hannah had been arrested by the sheriff and was being held in the county jail on a charge of murder. She had called my office and wanted me to come right away. I had underestimated our fat sheriff's appetite for genuine mischief.

At the country courthouse I set in motion my request for an early hearing on bail and went to see my incarcerated client. Hannah looked shattered and burst into tears when she saw me. I held her hand. It took a while for her to calm down enough to tell her story.

The sheriff had simply come by at six in the morning with a warrant and hauled her off. He asked her questions, after the usual Miranda, about her whereabouts on the morning of the murder, saying he had a witness that had seen her enter the Administration Building not long before the time of the murder. And he asked her about her father. Here she broke down again. She made a visible effort to get hold of herself.

"Sean," she said finally, "I've got to tell you a story I haven't told anybody here before. I never thought I would need to, and I know it has nothing to do with Bill's murder, but the sheriff thinks it does. He thinks I killed my husband to protect my father."

"Easy, Hannah," I said. "I've got all the time you need."
It did sound farfetched, but I have learned to listen.

"I was born in Germany," she began, catching her breath,
"in what is now the German Democratic Republic, in Leipzig. My father was in the SS. I was too young to understand
what it was all about, the Nazis, the war, the camps. When
the Russians came, my mother and I fled to West Germany.
My father had been captured by the Americans. He escaped
and went to Argentina and was later accused of being a
war criminal. We never saw him, but he sent word to my
mother where he was and wanted us to come to Argentina.
My mother refused to go, and we went to America with
the help of an intelligence officer in the American Occupation Forces."

"Bill?" I said.

She nodded, and tears welled up in her eyes again. "He
was very kind to us. He had questioned my father before
he escaped. It was his job to interrogate prisoners and
refugees. He could see that my mother was opposed to
everything the Nazis stood for, and he took pity on us.
We were sponsored by some friends of his in Massachu-
setts, and when he left the army to continue his graduate
work, he got in touch with us again. He was a kind of
hero to me, you can understand. Even though he was
older, we fell in love, and when I graduated from college,
we got married. My mother died two years later, and that
was the end of any family I knew, as far as I was concerned,
until two months ago, when I got a call from my father."
She stopped again to take a deep breath.

"It was a shock, and at first I didn't believe him. He
said not to tell my husband or anyone, but he was in the
United States and was very old and ill, and he wanted to
see me before he died. He sounded pitiful, but I said no.
He said he needed money, and he was going to die soon,
and the past was the past. I still said no and hung up.

"I told Bill, and he was distressed. He said he knew my father was in the United States because the army was still in contact with him and told him, but he decided not to tell me because he knew it would upset me. They were searching for him and thought he was living somewhere in New Jersey. Then my father called again three weeks ago and said the same thing. He needed money and was going to come and see me. He asked me if I had told my husband about his call, and I told him I had. He was furious and said Bill would turn him in to the FBI, that I was a traitor, and I hung up again. I told Bill about his second call."

She stopped again, putting her hands flat against her face. I waited. I wanted to give her a comforting hug, but under the circumstances, I couldn't. She needed someone to hold her, but that someone wasn't here anymore.

She dropped her hands to her lap. "I don't know how the sheriff found out about my father and his calls, but he knows. He thinks I killed Bill to prevent Bill from turning in my father." She looked straight at me with her reddened eyes and said in a firm voice, "I didn't kill him, Sean. I couldn't kill anyone, and certainly not the one person I loved more than anyone else in the world."

As she talked, I thought about the intelligence papers on Bill's desk, with the reference to the family of a war criminal living in Leipzig. How did that fit in? And had Bill informed the FBI about the calls, and they, in turn, the sheriff?

"You said the sheriff had a witness of some sort?" I said.

"He didn't say who, but someone claims to have seen me before two o'clock going into the Administration Building. Sean, I did not go to the campus until after two o'clock."

I had to find out who the witness, supposed witness, was. Another of Anderson's henchpersons? If there was a legitimate witness, it had to be a case of mistaking the time, or someone for Hannah. Had Hannah's father actually come to Silvertown? To do Bill in to protect himself?

I tried to reassure Hannah. I told her about the bail hearing and that I was confident we could have her out of jail very soon.

No more easy does it, I said to myself. I've got to get moving.

I wheeled my four-wheel drive (my Honda was being towed to the body shop, but I doubted that even a Jarvis heart could revive it) to the Silvertown Police Department.

"Are you all right?" Dicky asked. "The State Police spotted your car in the ditch."

"A few bruises and a wounded dignity," I said.

"I'm sorry about Hannah," he said. "I can't really believe she would murder her husband." The lines in his face had sunk even deeper. He looked the way he had when his wife died. Was something adding up for him, too?

"You had nothing to do with the arrest?"

"All the sheriff's doing," he said. "I was as surprised as you must have been."

"Okay," I said. "But I need to know a lot of things. First of all, what did you find out about my list of suspects?"

He gave me his report. Professor Wallace, with his claim to fame, had been arrested for trying to pick up a police woman dressed as a prostitute. Suspended sentence. And the date of the trial was the date of the murder. That was in Madison. A fair alibi. And, no doubt, the reason for his lies.

Acting Chancellor Hartpence had been picked up for drunken driving in Milwaukee. Case pending. (That might dampen the fires of enthusiasm for his elevation.)

The crime lab had turned up nothing on the bomb fragments or the warning note that was particularly helpful. Nick Lee had been arrested and convicted for possession of narcotics. He had been arrested for selling cocaine, and that case was pending. He was out on bail. That was from Milwaukee.

Dicky leaned back in his swivel chair and opined that maybe Nick was also a dealer in Silvertown.

I mentioned that Train had been on the Crime Commission and that the commission had been investigating drug trafficking.

"Maybe there's more to Nick's anger at the chancellor than being expelled," Dicky said.

"The work of the commission is supposed to be secret," I said, "but, of course, there may be leaks. I'm sure the Mafia would go to great lengths to develop sources of information about the commission's work."

"Would they take out a contract on Train simply because he's a member of the commission?" Dicky asked skeptically. He put his feet on his desk to think better.

"Nick Lee hardly seems professional enough for a contract man, even if the drug dealers thought the chancellor was a threat to their business."

"Well," Dicky said, "you shouldn't credit Mafia types with being as smart or as slick as they are portrayed. They do some dumb things and use dumb people sometimes."

"You mean like using Fountain and Fessler for hit men?" I said.

Dicky looked as though he had been hit himself. "Huh?" he said. "Fountain and Fessler?"

"I didn't drive into the ditch last night all on my own, Dicky. I was forced off the road by Fountain and Fessler. And they came after me to finish me off, only I was in the woods by then."

All the ridges in his face had turned pale. "Sean," he

158

said. "My God. I had nothing to do with that. I don't know what the hell is going on."

"I think you do, my friend. I find it hard to accept that you are involved with the sheriff's enterprises, whatever they all are, but you know. He has something on you."

Dicky shook his head. "My God," he said again.

"I'm going to lay it out, and I want some answers from you. Nick Lee is a dealer for the Black Mafia. Anderson is some kind of distributor, protector, contact man, capo, whatever, for the white Mafia. Fountain and Fessler are enforcers. Have I got it straight so far?"

Dicky had his thumb on one temple and his index finger on the other. "I guess so, Sean. I don't really know the details. I just guess."

"Have you been bought off, scared off, or are you a part of it? How did he get to you?"

"What are you going to do with all this?"

"Answer my question."

"All right, Sean. You want to know. It's very simple. Isabel. I bought some heroin for her off a dealer I had spotted in town. I didn't know then that Bert controlled the distribution of the stuff. I just wanted to help Isabel."

"The pain?"

"Yes. That last year was very bad, and Isabel begged me to get something."

"Didn't Doc Jensen have painkillers for her?"

"Yes, but they weren't doing the job. She wanted to try something stronger. She had heard someplace that they used heroin in England and other places perfectly legally for cancer pain in terminal patients. So I got some."

"And then you got more."

"Isabel said it helped."

"And then?"

"And then I got a visit from Bert Anderson."

159

"He told you what?"

"That his dealers would keep me supplied as long as I needed it, and that he didn't want me poking my nose in his business."

"And after Isabel died?"

"He held it over me still. My God, Sean, I hated myself, but I'd do it again for Isabel."

"O.K., I understand. Has he asked anything else of you?"

"Never. Just to keep my boys off him and his people."

"And you have."

"And I have." His eyes were wet. "I'm sorry, Sean."

"I am, too. But it's time to make a break. I need your help."

"What are you going to do? You can't take on that bully and his trigger-happy gun-toters."

"I don't intend to take him on myself. When the time comes, there are others who can do that job right. But I do intend to get Hannah out of this mess. I intend to find Bill's killer. If that process opens up Bert's operation, so be it. If Bert is somehow related to the murder, then I will go after him. Are you with me?"

"I'm at the end of my career anyway. I'm with you."

I let out a big sigh. It's not my style to let myself get all tensed up, but I was tight as a drum now. I wasn't sure whether my old friend Dicky James was really on my side or not. I had to take some chances.

I returned to my office, feeling the bruises and bumps of last night's acrobatics and little blips of apprehension in my brain for the future of Sean Fogarty, attorney at law, his family, and his clients.

The bail hearing had been set for late afternoon. Betty Olson had called again. I called back. She said the chancellor's office had been entered last night and files rifled. She knew because of the way the files were disarranged. She hadn't informed Hartpence because she was certain it

160

had to do with the murder and to what she had to show me. I really had to come to see her after she got home from work. I apologized for not having gone before and promised to go this evening. About drugs? I had drugs on my mind. I had a hunch Betty's information, whatever it was, would be useful. I hoped it would move me where I would have to go anyway.

# XXVI

With an hour before the bail hearing, I stopped by the university. I parked at the service entry of the Wall Memorial Art Building. Students were changing classes, coming from the foundry and the ceramics studio. I climbed to the third floor and saw Teddy Hughes emerging from a classroom. He saw me, turned his head away quickly, talking to a student. I waited. He turned slightly back toward me, catching me in his peripheral vision, I was sure. I waited, and as he walked along the corridor with the student, I said, "I need to talk to you, Teddy."

He nodded dumbly and said good-bye to the student. "My office?" he said to me then.

I nodded, and he led the way. It was hard for me to think that this slight, nervous man could be the Silvertown cocaine connection. But, then, what better disguise? And some effeminate men were, of course, as tough as some women.

We sat, and he looked at me expectantly.

"I'm learning things as I go along," I said.

He was still expecting. He brushed some hair from his eyes.

"You are aware that Chancellor Train was on the State Crime Commission?"

162

There was a small metamorphosis in his face. It seemed suddenly to age like the face of the young girl in *Lost Horizon* when she left the valley of Shangri-La.

"You know, I'm sure, that one of the matters—in fact, the first—they have begun to look into is the drug trade in this state."

He made no sign.

"As I think I told you before, I am not the police. I have not yet revealed who threw the pipe bomb through my window, though I have now come to understand that the reason I led you on to state may not be the actual reason you tried to warn me off. I am not the police, and I am not here to talk about the drug trade in Wisconsin, except as it may pertain to the murder of the chancellor. Now, if the chancellor came into possession of information about drugs being sold in Silvertown, in the university, he might very well make an effort to act on his information to stop this kind of activity. He might, for example, call you into his office and indicate that he had information that you were purveying cocaine and that he wanted you to stop or he would take certain actions."

There was still no response.

"Did he call you into his office recently to talk about drugs?"

"No, he didn't," Teddy said at last.

"He didn't talk to you, or didn't talk to you recently?"

"I hadn't talked to him in years."

"Years?"

He nodded. There was the beginning of a hard smile on his face.

"Did he talk to you years ago about drugs?"

"That's none of your damned business."

"That was before he was appointed to the Crime Commission?"

163

"He was appointed to the Crime Commission last year."

"So he knew about your activities long before?"

The slight hard smile remained.

"Did he warn you off?"

Teddy's expression remained unchanged, the smile, a cruel air of amusement.

I didn't want to ask it, but I did. "Did he buy drugs from you?"

The same sphinx.

"Is this drug business related in any way to his murder?"

No reply. He rubbed the back of his hand along the side of his nose.

"Do you know Nick Lee?"

His eyebrows went up a trifle. "I have nothing to do with Nick Lee," he said.

Given that he had refused to lie in answer to my previous questions, could I take it he was telling the truth in answer to this one? Anyway, Nick was his competitor, wasn't he?

"Did Fountain or Fessler make the pipe bomb for you to throw?"

He looked startled, then smiled.

"Teddy," I said, "I'm going to get to the bottom of this murder, and if it's connected to you and this damnable cocaine business, I'll get you, too."

He let loose a piping, cruel laugh. "You're a poor innocent little sheep," he said. "You're not scaring anybody."

"I may have been innocent," I said. "But let me tell you, I'm not a sheep."

I walked out, feeling lousy, not a sheep but a muttonhead. My little town of Silvertown. I knew, I had to know, there were people like Teddy and Nick Lee and Bert Anderson and Fountain and the rest of them, but breathing the same air at close range made me sick.

And what did I know now about Bill? Or Hannah, was

it Hannah and her long-sleeved dresses that I had learned about? Was everything I had thought I knew, I thought I had figured out about the murder, cockeyed and simple-minded? Had Train gotten a line on Anderson and Hughes and Fountain and Fessler and been silenced with a bronze abstraction?

# XXVII

The judge listened with a show of forbearance to the county prosecutor and then to me and set bail without hesitation at ten thousand dollars. He had made no comment during the hearing, but his manner (and I had had some experience in reading his every expression) suggested he hadn't much use for the prosecutor's case. He probably wasn't up on the depths to which the county sheriff could sink.

I had Hannah out in an hour and drove her to Lake Arrowhead to the Train house. It's a striking house, set into an incline, cantilevered over the lake shore, with lots of glass in an enormous living room, a large stone fireplace. The living room had been ideal for entertaining, and the Trains had entertained beautifully. The public relations part of the job.

A lonely house now. Hannah looked gaunt. She had been thrice injured of late: her father's reappearance, her husband's death by murder, her arrest for murder. Grief, the sense of injustice, comes over you like a wave, and recedes slowly. I remembered my father's death, the injustice of his treatment by the local money brokers.

I started a fire in the fireplace while Hannah made some coffee. I told her I thought my search for the murderer was coming to a close. She was surprised and asked who, but I said I would tell her when it all came out.

166

"All right," she said, and poured the coffee. It was not French roast, but it was good.

"A few more things from you, just to be sure."

She nodded.

"Did you know the Leibermans? Or did Bill know them before they came to Silvertown?"

She shook her head. "They were recommended by someone in State. I suppose Bill knew a lot about them."

"Bill was a member of the Crime Commission, you knew that?"

"Oh, yes. He had to go to Madison once a month for meetings. He said it was a kind of study group."

"That's their main purpose, but of course as they work they turn up concrete evidence of crimes. He never mentioned any names or anything specific about the work of the commission? For example, any connection with activities in Silvertown?"

"No. He just said they had a staff doing the legwork and that the extent of criminal activity was surprising to him."

"Did he mention anything about drugs?"

She shook her head. She looked even gaunter as I questioned her. I must sound like the sheriff, I thought. Little did she know how rotten he really was.

"I'm sorry to ask these questions," I said.

"You have to find out, don't you," she said, sadly. She tugged absently at the cuffs of her long sleeves.

I nodded. "I have to get everything as clear as I can, to make sure that I'm on the right track and that I am not sidetracked by irrelevant things."

She nodded. The fire crackled behind her. The lake over her shoulder was covered with rough ice, and wind was blowing wisps of snow over the surface. It could be Russia. You could almost expect troikas to appear running down the lake.

"The drug pipeline runs all over the state, even to Silvertown."

"Yes. I'm not surprised," she said.

"Bill said nothing about suppliers or dealers or anything of that sort in Silvertown, or anywhere?"

She shook her head.

"I know Bert Anderson asked you questions like this, but bear with me a while longer. Is there anything else in your or Bill's past that you know of that might have caught up with him?"

"I can't think of anything, Sean. But, of course, I did know Bill had done work for the government, so I suppose there could have been something. I didn't really know him then. He was a little older, you know, and he was a kind of romantic figure to me. He sort of swept me off my feet. He talked a little bit about his past. His parents were dead already. He had a brother somewhere—in England, I think— he didn't see very much and hadn't since they were young. My own life had not been very remarkable after we came to this country."

"Why did you and Bill come to Silvertown?"

"Because we were offered the job, I guess. No, that's not all. Bill came up to look at the campus incognito before we were even interviewed. He loved it. We had always talked about building a house on a lake somewhere, and he said this was the place. He liked his job. He was contacted about other jobs several times while we were here, especially the first ten years—the first time only six months after we were here—but he wasn't interested. We loved it here. We intended to retire here in our house." Her eyes clouded, and she stopped talking for a while.

"I won't pry anymore," I said.

We talked a little more, quietly, and hugged each other. I took some of her pain with me. And even more pain, as I had to consider all the possibilities. Had Hannah actually entered the Administration Building the first time, when she entered alone, before two o'clock? At one or one-thirty, for example, within the time range Doc Jensen had opined that the murder could have been committed? Had I been blind to that possibility because of my affection for Hannah?

# XXVIII

I called Betty Olson from my office at five-thirty. She said I could come by then. She sounded nervous. She lived in a small white house beside the Methodist Church. She had to unlock the door to the house and then the screened-in porch to let me in. A padded New England rocker faced the television set. On a table beside the rocker was a worn Bible. I sat in an overstuffed chair at an angle to the television, which was still on. She turned it off and sat in her rocker.

"You said, if I withheld information about a murder, I could be prosecuted as an accessory after the fact." She had her hand on the Bible.

"That's true," I said.

"I don't know whether what I have is that kind of information or not. I mean, I don't know whether it is related to the chancellor's death, but I think so."

"Why don't you just tell me."

"It's here," she said. She lifted the Bible and brought out a sheet of paper. She handed it to me as I rose to accept it.

"It's just a poem," she said. "But I think I know where it came from and who wrote it. And I think she broke into the files to get it."

It was indeed a poem, handwritten. A romantic poem,

as I remembered from reading Shelley in my college days, flowery, stilted with thees and thous, a declaration of undying love.

"It was at the bottom of a file drawer," Betty said. "I was cleaning out the files in Dr. Train's desk as Dr. Hartpence asked me to, and this had slipped down under the file folders. Then I found a file folder I think it might have been in, but the contents were missing. There was nothing at all in it."

"Why do you think the poem came from that folder?"

"It was the only empty folder in the drawer."

"What was the heading on the folder?"

She reached under her Bible again and brought forth a folder. I rose to take it, and read on the tab: PR.

"Polly Rector," Betty said.

"You think the chancellor had a file of poems by Polly Rector?" I said.

"Interoffice envelopes used to come maybe once a month marked confidential. The chancellor never put their contents or anything relating to them in the out box to be filed in the outer office."

"So he must have filed the contents himself."

"Yes, sir."

"Did you figure out where the envelopes came from?"

She blushed a little. "Yes, sir."

"How did you do that?"

"I watched to see the crossed-out names above. The interoffice envelopes have space for a whole lot of names. The user simply crosses out the name above and addresses it to another person. It saves money."

"And you read the crossed-out name each time."

She nodded. "It was always someone in the English Department."

"It could have been anyone in the English Department."

She shook her head. She pointed to the poem in my

hand. "That poem is in Polly Rector's book." She put her hand back on the Bible table and brought forth the thin magenta book.

*The Cry of the Dove,* by Polly Rector, published by the Maple Tree Press, dedicated "To the defender of my dreams." I read the title of the poem Betty had found and the list in the index and found the page. The same. "As long as I live/As long as thou livest/Thou hast my love," the last lines read.

"You have done the right thing, Mrs. Olson," I said.

"My husband worked for your father," she said, "in the paper mill."

"I didn't know that," I said.

"He was a foreman there until the mill closed. Twenty years."

"What did he do then?"

"He went to work in Milwaukee. Then when he retired, we came back up here. He died ten years ago."

"I can understand why you came back," I said.

"It was too bad about the mill," she said. "And your father."

"Yes," I said. I thanked her, gave her back the book, and she let me through the two doors, with the poem and the folder, and locked them after me.

As long as I lived, I would love my father, I thought. But it's not relevant to this story. He lost the mill because it was small and needed modernizing. The banks wouldn't back him. People lost their jobs, and he lost something as valuable to himself, but he persevered, worked his way back, buying timber and keeping us together. He died doing it, pushing to make a future for us.

Undying romantic love was something different. Glandular hyperbole. I drove to Hickory Street, a mile down from Betty Ransom's apartment, a better neighborhood, still white and red Victorian houses. Polly lived in a rambling one story with rooms added and porches tacked on over the years by its previous owner. I had been there once a long time ago for a party. That was before the suit against the city. Her lights were on. I knocked. Her dog went into a spasm of barking. She swore at it.

She peered through the window at the side of the door before she opened it. "I've been wondering when you would come back to see me," she said. She ordered her dog into another room.

"I had to be sure," I said.

"Come into the study," she said. "It's more comfortable."

I followed her. The study was totally lined with books except for the window and doors. She thumped across the wood floor to a big chair and sat down heavily. I sat across from her in a small leather side chair. I reached across the space between us and handed her the poem.

"You took one piece of paper, but you left another," I said.

She looked at the poem, and her eyes clouded. "I loved him, you know."

"I know."

"It's unbelievable, isn't it," she said, her voice growing hoarse. "An ugly, fat woman nursing a secret love for fifteen years."

"All of us love," I said. "No matter."

"An impossible love."

"That happens, too."

"I sent him lots of these. This one a long time ago, years before the book was published. I wrote it for him."

"He was the defender of your dreams?"

"Yes. I tried to make him that anyway."

"When you went to see him that day, what did you intend?"

"Only to ask for my poems back. I didn't know whether

173

he had saved them or thrown them away. But I wanted them back. Maybe I just wanted to see him."

"And you found him there with the intelligence papers."

"Yes. They were on his conference table. I had surprised him. He had just gotten them, I think. A man in a dark suit was walking out of the building when I entered. I think he must have brought them."

"You accused him of betraying his values by doing that kind of work for the government?"

"He was a spy. Those CIA types, you know what they have done, violating everything decent and moral . . ." She broke off.

"He defended himself?"

"No. He didn't say anything. He . . . just sat there. I told him I wanted my poems back. He said he would give them to me. He got them out of his file and took them from a folder and gave them to me, just like that."

"What happened then?"

"I don't know. I tried to put my arms around him. I asked him to hold me just once. I humiliated myself, can you understand? I don't know what came over me. I wanted to humiliate myself, a kind of vengeance on myself for being romantic and stupid, for being a victim of this crazy passion."

"He wouldn't hold you?"

"He pushed me away. He told me to get hold of myself. I kept trying to embrace him, I was unhinged, I cried and tried and tried to . . ."

She started to cry.

I waited.

"He rejected me, and I don't know what happened. It's a crazy blur. I was furious then. The spy papers were on his conference table. I ran to the table and scattered them all over. I screamed at him. He tried to stop me. Now he was holding me; he had hold of my arms, shaking me. I kissed him. His face was revulsed. I began beating on his chest, and he held my arms. Oh Christ, I wanted him to love me, and he was revulsed. I am so ugly." Her face was contorted with anguish, and the tears were running down her fat cheeks in streams; her body shook like blubber.

"I don't know what happened. He started to lead me to the door. I think he would have pushed me out. I said I was all right. I calmed down. He asked me to leave. He turned to lead me to the door again and I picked up the sculpture and hit him. He fell like a log. The phone rang and scared me. I made myself think. Be calm and think. I got some Kleenex from my purse and wiped my fingerprints off everything, and I took my poems, which I had put down on the conference table. I gathered my poems, and someone knocked at the door. It was Hannah, and she called his name. I was panicked. I waited, and she went away. I took my poems and went down the elevator to the basement and put it on hold to keep people from going up, and went to my office. When I calmed down and went to put my poems away, I found the paper, the spy paper."

She stopped and caught her breath, wiped her tears and nose on the sleeve of her flowing dress.

"Sean, I loved him."

"You fought with him all the time."

"Because I loved him. I wanted him to do what he should. He didn't know what was going on, what his dean of instruction was doing, what his deans were doing. If he had listened . . ."

"And for all those years you loved him and sent him poems."

"Yes. There were hundreds of poems. They were all for him. When I first sent one, I wasn't sure he would know it was from me, but he guessed. I told him I was a poet, and he said he knew, but he didn't say anything more. It went on and on. He was the one I loved, and he was someone else. In my fantasy he was my lover; in reality he was that man who ignored me. I went to see him and tell him what was going on, so that he could take action. He would listen and smile, and that was all. That was all. Everything. I am crazy. I am crazy as Ahab. He was everything I wanted, and he took it away. They bore him barefaced on the bier. Hey non nonny, hey nonny. I killed myself, didn't I? And will he not come again? No, no, he is dead. It's gone, isn't it? Everything is gone." She looked at me then. She had been talking as though I were not really there.

I nodded. "Yes, Polly. It's all gone now."

"What will we do?"

"We will call Dicky James," I said.

"Not the sheriff."

"No, not the sheriff."

"Now?"

"It's time."

"All right."

I went to the phone on her desk and called Dicky James and asked him to come with someone to take notes. "Better here," I said.

"Sean," Polly said, "I'm sorry."

"So am I, Polly."

She was quivering in a sea of tears.

# XXIX

It was a long night. I called Susie, and she put supper back in the oven. Dicky was good, as I knew he'd be. He had gone home from work, but came to deal with Polly himself. He brought Officer Dawson and a tape recorder. He warned Polly; she waived her right to an attorney, saying I was present anyway. She said she wanted me to act as her attorney. I pointed out there was a conflict of interest, since I had been the one who had tracked this case through. She said she would need an attorney in court and wanted me to act. To smooth things along, I said I would, if the court approved.

She talked matter-of-factly into the tape recorder, and Dicky and Dawson then took her downtown to the police station.

Susie hugged me when I got home.

"It's all over, isn't it?" she said.

"Yes," I said. I kissed her thankfully.

I called Hannah, and she was relieved, but grieved all over again at the senselessness of Bill's death.

We had a late supper, and I told Susie the whole thing.

"You had it figured from early on, didn't you?" Susie said, pushing away her empty plate and leaning on her pretty elbows.

"Well, I was fairly sure from the time Polly gave me

177

that missing spy page, but I had some doubts along the way."

"Somebody else could have taken that page and given it to Polly, as she hinted."

"Why would someone who had taken the paper have given it to Polly? And why would Polly protect such a person, if he or she were possibly guilty of murder? It had to be Polly."

"Why did she give *you* that page?"

"She thought she was sending me off on a blind trail. If we all came to believe it was the CIA and they wouldn't talk, the heat would be dissipated. Then, again, maybe she wanted to be caught. When I showed her the poem Betty Olson found, she almost seemed relieved. I think perhaps she wanted me to find out. She wanted to get it off her bosom."

"You said all along it might be love, that maybe Bill had a girlfriend."

"Yuk."

"What about that spy business? What was Bill really doing?"

"I guess we'll never know for sure, but I think he was a kind of consultant. Anyway, the fact that their courier—I assume that's what he was—was on campus that day meant he was either delivering or picking up the papers. That had to mean the missing page was pilfered on that day, I thought. The coincidence of the agent's presence and the murder suggested the agent might have done it, but the missing paper suggested the secret document was simply a target of opportunity."

"What about Wallace, Richards, Lee, Hartpence, and Penney? Didn't you suspect them?"

"I suspected everybody with a motive. Wallace turns out to have been in court in Madison, being convicted of feeling up a policewoman under the impression she was a prostitute."

It was Susie's turn to say "Yuk." Then she added, "There is some justice at least."

"As for Hartpence, if he did away with his first wife, he did so cleverly. Why would he stoop to bludgeoning the chancellor? It would have been out of character for him to try to take Bill on physically.

"Richards I worried about because he had a big cause, but I concluded he was more of an opportunist than an Indian. And Penney was worth his name. I eliminated everybody finally, except Polly."

"What about the sheriff's witness?"

"The witness saw Polly."

"But Polly is fat."

"Both Polly and Hannah are tall. The witness probably saw a tall woman with a loose coat on at a distance. Witnesses remember what they think they were going to see, anyway. I think it was Polly, and when I heard about there being a witness, it helped to confirm my belief that it had to be Polly. I just needed a key to get to her. Betty Olson gave me that."

"Pickel and the old alums?"

"Those guys can't even get their jockstraps on straight."

"Nick Lee?"

"He's angry and violent enough, and when all that information began to come together about drugs, I began to wonder about our very own, our native Mafia. If I could have satisfied myself some other way about the missing page, I probably would have gone for a theory about a drug killing. By the way, have you ever seen Hannah in short sleeves?"

"Why on earth do you ask that?"

"I just wondered."

179

"You don't just wonder anything. Good God, you think Hannah shoots up?"

"The thought entered my mind. Her long sleeves. I thought Bill might have known about Teddy's drug dealing, yet he hadn't turned him in."

"Oh, Sean, how could you?" Susie was distressed. "I saw Hannah in a swim suit at the university pool at community swims. No needle marks. I didn't look specially, but I would have noticed. Sean, you're terrible."

"I guess you're right. Finding out these things about Silvertown's inhabitants has warped my view of humanity."

"We're not all like that. Anyway, it's all over now. How about coming to bed with this innocent inhabitant?"

"Polly has asked me to defend her."

"Sean, that's impossible. You can't do that. Isn't that a conflict of interest, or something?"

"That's what I've tried to say."

"That's crazy. Just say no. You're not everybody's knight errant."

"I feel like I've been fighting infidels with a slingshot."

"What are you going to do about the sheriff and the drug gang?"

"Them I'm not going to take on. I'll call Jane Ayre in the morning and tell her what I know. She'll know who to sic on them."

"You have to be a witness then."

"I'll be a witness."

"You'll have to be careful till it's all over."

"I'll be careful. I think Dicky James will help me now."

"What about Dicky James?"

"I'm not going to rat on Dicky. When a man loves his wife like that, you have to forgive him."

"Would you break the law for me?"

"I'd undo the Constitution for you."

After that we went to bed.

# XXX

Silvertown was abuzz the next day. My phone was ringing with people wanting to know all about it. Reporters from Madison and Milwaukee called, wanting details. Dicky James had apparently revealed my role in uncovering the identity of the murderer. I referred everyone back to him. I went to see Polly in jail. It was impossible to get anything done at the office, and I went home early, walking in fresh spring air. You have to catch that when you can. I was depressed. My Silvertown, America. I felt bereaved all over again for Bill and for Hannah. And for Polly. And for the victims of our drug racket.

I had tried again to persuade Polly that, because of my activities in searching out the murderer, it was inappropriate for me to serve as her attorney. She again insisted. She had confidence in my fairness and my skill. And what did it matter? She had confessed. She had done it.

If I were actually going to defend the person I had unveiled—who had unveiled herself to me—as the murderer of my friend, I had to begin thinking very differently. (Why me? I had enough trouble smoking her out.) She had a right to a fair trial and to a vigorous defense. How would she plead? I had to begin to think about the strange fantasy that had led to the killing. She had said, and I believed her, that she had not intended to kill Bill when

181

she went to his office. It was not premeditated. We would wait to see what the formal charges were. I would ask for a reasonable bail. She was unlikely to find another fantasy lover soon. Or an appropriate piece of sculpture.

In her confession to me, which was more elaborate and personal than her official confession to Dicky James, she had quoted from Shakespeare, lines—if my English-major recollections were correct—from Ophelia's deranged singing about the death of Polonius, her father, who had been accidentally but callously killed by her lover, Hamlet. Did she think of herself as Ophelia? Why should lines from Ophelia's sad maunderings about her father's death find their way into Polly's confession? Did Polly think of her fantasy lover as her father when she killed him? Was she truly crazy, after all? Or at the time of the murder? She said she was crazy as Ahab. Searching obsessively for romantic love? Or was it literary nonsense, to prepare a defense of having lost her senses?

I called Jane Ayre to report on my discoveries about drugs in Silvertown. She said she would notify the attorney general's office. They would get in touch with me. Himself called back within the hour. He called me "Sean" (we met once at a Bar meeting) and said the State Police would get on it right away. I hoped the sheriff would stay off it until the State Police got on it.

Susie decided we should go out to cheer me up. We went to Jolly's, of course. We ordered steaks, one rare, one well done, and sipped our Scotch and wine as we waited.

"I never did get to interview Women's Studies," I said.

Susie pinched me on the biceps. "I think you really enjoyed playing detective."

The fact of the matter was I did, but I wasn't sure how Susie would react to that. I figured I'd better wait for more clues from her. "Well . . . ," I said.

"Fess up," she said.

"I suppose I did," I conceded the point. "But of course that was a one-time thing, so you needn't worry. After all, how many murders get committed in Silvertown?"

"Probably more than we suspect," Susie said. Was she egging me on? Then she touched my shin with her foot. "Here comes Nate Colby," she said.

Nate Colby stopped by our table. I resisted the respectful urge to stand.

"Mr. Fogarty," he said. He held out his hand.

"Mr. Colby," I said. We shook.

He nodded at Susie. "Mrs. Fogarty," he said.

"Mr. Colby," she said.

"Congratulations," he said to me.

"Thank you," I said.

"A clever piece of sleuthing," he said.

"Thank you," I said.

He shook his head. "That poor woman," he said.

"Yes," I said. "That poor woman. And poor Bill Train."

He hesitated a moment. "Yes," he said. "Poor Bill."

He nodded at both of us. "Have a good dinner."

"Thank you," we said.

When he was out of earshot, Susie said, "I'm proud of you, Sean."

"What did I do now?"

"You were restrained and polite. Actually, you despise the bastard, don't you?"

"I'm always restrained and polite."

Susie smiled.

"And how was your day?"

"Fine," she said. "Cathy called."

"Again while I was not at home? What now?"

"She's met another boy."

"So soon?"

"So it seems."

"Another pre-med?"

"A drama major from Yale."

"A *drama* major from *Yale*? Ye gods."

Susie nodded. "Um hm," she said. "He's in rehearsal for *Camelot*."

"For *Camelot*?"

Susie nodded.

"Then she's staying?"

"Yes, she's staying."

"This one had better treat her right, or I'll kill him," I said.

Susie smiled.